Foreword

by "Dinosaur" George Blasing

Mark is one of those rare authors who possess the ability to create a story that is so intriguing, you find yourself becoming immersed in every page.

The Fourth Queen and The Lost Queen send readers on mythical tales of excitement, fantasy and drama. Each book is filled with vivid imagery of a magical land of wonder and peril. And his use of positive female role models is a welcome change to the stereotypical characters we often find in print. It is so refreshing to read a story where honesty, courage and honor are rewarded while wickedness and deceit are met with failure.

But of all of his works, The Secret Queen is indeed the crown jewel, so far. This book does a fantastic job of interweaving drama and storylines, while injecting some "prehistoric" characters the readers will love. The Secret Queen incorporates science with fantasy to create such mesmerizing characters as Baharians based on an actual dinosaur, Bahariasaurus. Or Carcharodans, modeled after the deadly predator of the late cretaceous landscape of Egypt; Carcharodontosaurus. The readers will be taken to a world where Parasauratitan, Majungahan and Spinolock each have their part in this mythical world of wonder.

As a paleontologist, I am so impressed with Mark's ability to create his fictional characters around actual dinosaurs, and then bring them to life in his amazing storytelling ability. And his descriptive writing style allows the reader to quickly identify the factual inspiration behind each dinosaur character. I am so happy that he chose such a unique variety of dinosaur species. Many authors who incorporate dinosaurs into their works often utilize only the most common species. Mark chooses to weave some lesser known, yet very exciting, species of dinosaurs into his story.

Mark's writing style makes his stories easy to read and understand for any age. For young and old, girls or boys, everyone who has the good fortune to read his books will find that they are hard to put down. And parents can purchase with confidence knowing that every story is written with decency, respect and integrity by a father who loves his daughters.

With its cast of positive role models, evil forces and dinosaur based characters, The Secret Queen is sure to be a hit with readers of all ages. I am thrilled to be a part of such exciting and thrilling stories that demonstrate the virtues of honesty and morals.

What others are saying about Mark Miller's writing...

"...a well-crafted piece of literature with many unexpected twists and turns throughout..."

-Amazon Review

"Miller has a lot of whatever it is that makes a good fantasy writer...Whatever the secret is to writing great fantasy, The Secret Queen is the result."

-Reader's Favorite Book Reviews

"There is a musical quality to the way Miller writes that makes the reader want to pick up more of his books. Something else that should be considered is that these books have very strong female protagonists, none of the wimpy ones we see too often nowadays, so it's a great choice for teen girls."

-Midwest Book Reviews

"From trials and victories, battles and moments of heartwarming scenarios, The Fourth Queen is a novel the entire family will find enjoyable... His vivid and descriptive narratives portray him as a master of the craft."

-Amazon Review

Books by
Mark Miller

The Empyrical Tales
> Book I: Journey of the Fourth Queen
> Book II: Search for the Lost Queen
> Book III: Mystery of the Secret Queen
> Book IV: History of the First Queen

Small World Global Protection Agency
> #001 New Kids on the Rock
> #002 Bulls and Burglars
> #003 The Not So Perfect Game

Promise of Tomorrow

THE EMPYRICAL TALES BOOK III

MYSTERY OF THE SECRET QUEEN

Mark Miller

MillerWords, LLC

MillerWords, LLC
PO Box 861074
Shawnee, KS 66286

First Edition

For discounts on bulk purchases, please contact MillerWords Educational Sales at **Sales@MillerWords.com**

Printed in the United States of America

2 4 6 8 10 9 7 5 3 1

Library of Congress Control Number: 2018904439

ISBN: 978-0-9996195-4-4

For my Olena

Special Thanks to

"Dinosaur" George Blasing

Chapter 1

A eran the hawk perched on the thick cedar beam that spanned the top of the sandstone arch. The splintered wood left an odd sensation on his old wound. His long lost talons would never grow back.

Being smaller than the fearsome native hawks of this strange land, Aeran roosted unnoticed. He pecked momentarily at the wood beneath his claws hoping to find a snack. When he found no insects, he turned his attention back to the crowded marketplace.

He scanned the rows of tables shaded by their brightly colored awnings and tried to watch the hundreds of tanned faces that conducted their business today. Most of the market-goers were human, but the ones that made Aeran nervous had the heads and tails of cats attached to human bodies. Still, he did not spy the one wretched face he grew to know so well over the past several days. This made him wonder if the other innocent people could sense the evil in their midst.

The Captain of the Guardian Hawks stretched his wings, trying to ignore the dull ache of his year old injuries. This made him think of his tail feathers. Thankful that they, at least, had finally grown back, with some help from the Empyrical Wizards, he fanned them. Unfortunately, he still had nightmares of the black beast that chased him all the way from the eastern Palace by the Sea back to Castle Empyrean. With the excitement of the battle that followed, Aeran believed the ordeal had not traumatized him and the bad dreams were gone. Now, almost a year later, the nightmares returned.

In his recurring dream, more of the smoky black creatures escaped from the dark places across Empyrean, places he did not even recognize. He felt these unusual settings were places that no good creature or human would dare to venture. Then, each time he awoke from the nightmare, he could not shake the feeling that it actually happened. His only relief came from the fact that none of his hawks had reported any sightings or encounters with these creatures as they sailed over Empyrean.

He did get one report that piqued his interest, the report that eventually brought him to the land of the Southern Valley. In a year's time, he had learned much about being a leader. Some of the wizards even complimented him on it. One thing he learned was not to believe every story that winged its way into the aerie at the highest tower of Castle Empyrean. So many random, and false, stories made it to his nest. Aeran had learned to sort the truth from the fiction. That is why he doubted this tale at first.

Too many factors told his instincts that it could not be true. First, the object of the story was a rare gift of bird legend. Second, the original teller of the tale was a vulture. From personal experience, he found it difficult, at best, to believe vultures. In his estimation, a vulture would say anything to ensure its next meal. Thirdly, the vulture came from the Eurphoric Mountains. Again, from his own experience, Aeran knew the power of the Euphoric Mountains. He had flown through the treacherous passes of purple and gray stone. He felt the rush of euphoria that caused deliriousness and forgetfulness. Those mountains had an effect on any man or beast that passed through them. He highly doubted the accuracy of information from anyone that actually lived among those mountains.

Still, something about the report caused him to linger on it. The Captain spent several days considering the possibility. He wanted so badly for the story to be true, he did not dare name the object, even too himself. If he allowed himself hope and then found the story to be a lie, it would be too painful. Instead, he decided only to refer to it as the object.

That made it only slightly difficult to explain his decision to his fellow hawks. Aeran's nest mate, Fleta, heard the story directly from the vulture. As such, only she knew the details that caused Aeran such grief. When he looked upon her beauty, her penetrating black eyes and the golden feathers of her wings, he found strength. While they had only been together a short time, he knew they would stay together and he could trust her completely.

He perched before the rest of the hawks and explained, without truly explaining, that he would personally be going to discover the truth of the story. Relief washed over him when not one of the hawks questioned his decision. Several of the birds even volunteered to help, without knowing what may happen.

Derek, Bellevue and Habrok were not only three of the fastest hawks at Empyrean, but also three of Aeran's oldest friends. It made Aeran proud that they were among the few that volunteered.

Since then, their journey led them first to the Euphoric Mountains to investigate the original claim. After, they travelled into the east by way of a town called Bond. Supposedly, the object had been moved from its hiding place. Eventually, the clues and rumors led them to the Southern Valley. Everything Aeran learned seemed to point them toward one man. Finally, in the massive southern capital city of Hierakonpolis, they found proof of the object.

Worse than that, they found the man. Aeran discovered Spynum Begg, a twisted being intent on doing evil with the object. Aeran and his fellow hawks watched Spynum Begg for several days, so much that Aeran could recount the pattern of warts on what he considered to be a quite wretched face. They learned that whatever Begg planned to do with the object, he was going to do it at the marketplace near the home of the Queen of the Southern Valley, the Infinity Temple.

It seemed that Spynum Begg enjoyed some type of diplomatic status that allowed him to pass in and out of the Infinity Temple at his whim. This bothered Aeran because his instincts told him that Begg was a bad man. He did not like the idea of such a villain having free access to the temple while Queen Isis remained at Castle Empyrean so far away.

Now Aeran waited for the three other birds to find their assigned places in the market. Today, the captain planned to make history and he knew he could not let his pride get the better of him. That nearly cost him his life once before.

On the far side of the market, Aeran spotted Bellevue. He could see the slightly older hawk attempting to land near a particularly clumsy human. The human had constructed a flimsy looking device made mostly of thin sticks. Apparently, Bellevue must have thought it was intended to be a perch. From his spot, Aeran could not tell what it was supposed to be. All he could see was the skinny young man trying to awkwardly swat at Bellevue while also making a speech to the few market goers interested enough to slow down.

"Ladies and Gentle," he started. Then he stopped to take a swing at the hawk. "Ladies and Gentleman, my name is Lumpkin, Karl

Lumpkin." He turned back to Bellevue. "You're ruining it."

The idea of Bellevue attracting so much attention frustrated Aeran, but at the same time, it amused him. He guessed Bellevue, as stubborn as he was, had decided that the top of the boy's wobbly structure was the only place he could settle.

A few people slowed to watch the antics. The boy, Karl Lumpkin, must have thought they were interested in his display. Aeran cocked his head sideways to listen.

"Ah, you see," said Karl.

Aeran did not think much of Karl's presentation style.

"This is, what I have here. This." Karl waived his arms in a grand sweeping gesture. He brushed one thin branch of the haphazard criss-cross of narrow sticks. For a moment, Aeran thought the boy would collapse his own creation. The vibrations apparently forced Bellevue back into the air as well.

Karl Lumpkin continued, "This is my invention to revolutionize farming as you know it. I am a self-taught alchemist and free-thinker of old." Aeran thought the boy was trying to sound eloquent, but failing. "In my sixteen and three quarter years of life, I have travelled from the expansive forests of the Northern Wood across the dry deserts of the Southern Valley." Aeran could tell from the boy's clothes that he was not a southerner, but the style did not match the north either. He wore a vest like the kind favored by many westerners. Maybe he has travelled, thought Aeran, but he was still a boy.

While Aeran considered Karl Lumpkin's origins, Bellevue came to rest again. Again the boy swatted at him. More people stopped to watch the antics.

"You see. This method, my method, will change your life," Karl said.

Aeran could not take anymore. He knew Bellevue was attracting too much attention. He let out one shrill cry whose meaning was understood instantly by Bellevue. The bird darted away from the table as Karl took one last swing. Instead of focusing on his target, the boy turned to look in Aeran's direction. This left him off balance and he crashed into his own table. The entire mesh of sticks burst apart, flying in different directions. Many of the pieces landed on nearby merchants. One plopped in a large kettle of some kind of soup. The rest spilled down on top of Karl.

The onlookers chuckled before moving to the next booth. Aeran did not like to see what happened, but he knew a human's embarrassment was a small price to pay for their mission. He watched Karl start to gather the sticks, then stop to push his glasses back up on his thin nose.

Aeran confirmed that Bellevue found a new location, this time much less conspicuous. He then switched his attention to Derek, who apparently had been ready and in position for quite some time. This left only Habrok to occupy the fourth corner of the market. Once he was in place, they would be positioned to see every angle of the market.

However, Aeran could not find Habrok. Instead, in the spot where Habrok should have been, Aeran spotted a long serpent wrapped around an upright post. It had a few feathers sticking out of the corner of its mouth. The tan color with black speckles was unmistakable to Aeran. He knew Habrok's colors too well.

Despair set in quickly. He could not believe Habrok, the best of hawks, would allow himself to be eaten by a snake. Snakes of every kind enjoyed a place of honor here and Aeran did not like this about the Southern Valley. Cobras, asps and pythons of every size roamed free throughout even the smaller cities. In Hierakonpolis, the wealthy kept them as pets as well. At least, Aeran thought, the cat-people had the decency not to eat a bird. But they did always seem to have that hungry look in their eyes. Sadly, it appeared the snakes had no decency at all.

Now, Aeran had lost a dear friend and that also jeopardized their plan.

Before Aeran completely surrendered his quest, he caught a glimpse of more tan feathers with black speckles. Thankfully, these feathers remained attached to their owner. Atop the high block wall, Habrok nursed the tip of his wing. Relief filled Aeran as he realized Habrok must have narrowly missed becoming lunch. The bird roosted well out of reach of the python. He appeared to be okay, aside from the few missing feathers.

The distress and commotion could not have ended at a better time. Derek gave the signal that meant he spotted Spynum Begg on his side of the market. Almost in a panic, Aeran sprang into the air. He tried to get a vantage to see Begg, but could not immediately pick him out of the crowd. He believed things would soon be at a conclusion.

Then Bellevue swooped low over Karl Lumpkin's head. The boy had gathered up several pieces of his failed experiment only to drop them as Bellevue tussled his shaggy, brown hair in passing. Aeran tracked Bellevue's path directly toward their wicked prey.

Spynum Begg shouldered his way through the crowd with a large object tucked up under one arm. He kept it unceremoniously wrapped in a plain cloth. The Captain of the Guardian Hawks dared not hope it was the object of their quest. He did not want to find out what Begg had planned for it.

Aeran watched the man move with a purpose. His unnaturally hunched back did not seem to draw much attention in the diverse crowd. The hawk, however, felt repulsed by the man's face. He could not imagine trying to eat with so many warts so close to his mouth like Begg's. No one around him seemed to mind though. The size of the hidden object seemed to throw the skinny man off balance. He kept bumping into tables or other people. One cat woman hissed at him as he knocked over her display of jewelry.

The only thing that mattered to Aeran now was recovering the object that Spynum Begg held onto so desperately. It did not matter to the hawk if anyone else even noticed the man. The whole plan centered on Aeran and his hawks capturing the object. Maybe, Aeran thought, it was not the object he expected, but whatever it was, Begg apparently did not have an honest purpose for it.

The hawks circled Begg at a distance, waiting for an opportunity. When Aeran saw Begg approaching a secluded corner of the market, he gave the signal to act. The four birds dove in perfect unison, claws extended to capture the bundle of cloth. Begg looked up at his attackers at the last moment. This allowed him to duck out of the way.

Aeran recovered the fastest and turned for another pass. He saw Begg moving as fast as his wooden leg would allow. Derek, Bellevue and Habrok centered in behind him and Aeran knew they would be able to stop Begg.

Suddenly, Begg stopped on his own. He turned and ripped loose the cloth around the object. A swirling, oily mass of black smoke burst out of the cloth. He felt the pure evil of the creature as he hurled uncontrollably toward it. His mind froze as he recognized this horror as the same formless beast that chased him halfway across Empyrean and tormented his dreams. Before he could react, he and his comrades smashed into the creature and disappeared forever.

Except, this did not happen. Aeran, nor any of his hawks, were swallowed by the monster. Begg did not stop running and he did not hold one of those dark beasts under the cloth. All of that happened in Aeran's over-stressed imagination. However, he did almost slam into a table in his daze.

He righted himself at the last moment. Then he flapped his wings hard enough to feel the muscles burn. He watched Begg pass through the archway that marked one of the market exits and make a sharp turn out of sight.

The captain could not allow the vile man to escape. He swooped through the arch and made an equally sharp turn. This time he did not imagine the waiting surprise. He almost flew directly into an enormous mouth. He pulled up as the jagged teeth snapped closed. He looked back to make certain his friends did not meet that fate either. The other birds looked startled, but safe.

From his new height, Aeran could see the animal that almost ate him. This creature looked different than any he had encountered previously. At first, he thought it was some kind of bird. It stood on two legs, but was as big as a horse. Although scales covered most of its body, it had feathers around its head and along its long tail. As birdlike as it seemed, it had no wings, only short, clawed arms. Aeran had never known a bird to have arms, or teeth either. Nasty looking sharp teeth lined something that resembled a beak which had almost been his final resting place. Aeran now saw two more of these creatures nearby.

Then he realized Begg was not running to meet these strange bird animals. These unusual creatures wore saddles. Begg apparently came to meet the riders of these animals.

The four hawks landed safely on a nearby roof. They watched helplessly as Spynum Begg handed the covered object over to one of the riders. He did not look back at the birds, seemingly unconcerned as to why they were chasing him. The rider that accepted the package looked like a man, but he had green skin and narrow slit eyes, like a snake. However, they looked nothing like the snake-headed people of Hierakonpolis. His scales seemed to cover his whole body. The rider licked his lips with his forked tongue, which made Aeran understand he was definitely some type of reptile and definitely not from Empyrean.

The three riders mounted their beasts and left Begg with a large pouch of gold coins that spilled out on the ground. Begg showed his true greed as he scrambled in the dirt to collect them.

Aeran watched the riders head south, out of sight of the other market goers. He guessed they were heading for the southern border to lands beyond the reach of the four queens. As they rode away, the cloth slipped off the object.

The Captain of the Guardian Hawks felt both elated and utterly defeated. He now knew the story was true. He had it almost in his claws and lost it.

Aeran saw the egg.

Chapter 2

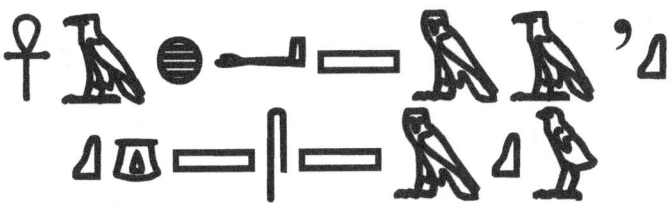

Olena spent her days continually in training. Even after a year, she felt like she had so much to learn. This both excited her and frustrated her.

She did not believe a seven-year-old should be forced into day after day of learning, but here she sat. Some days, it felt like a kind of torture. Before she became queen, Olena spent her time playing on the beach in Banookanook with her sister. These days, she had no playtime, no beach, and more so lately, no Zandria.

Zandria always seemed to be going off on some adventure with Adam or her elf friend, Dew Lantisphere. She could barely keep track of Zandria. She knew they would not have playtime again. Let alone playtime, Olena could not remember the last time she shared a meal with her sister.

Olena believed Zandria's missions must be important. Last year, she even saved their mother from the crystal prison called the Trammeler. Olena found and lost her mother on the same day because of that. That remained one of the happiest and saddest days of her life. Still, it did not affect

her in the same way that she thought it affected Zandria.

After that day, Zandria seemed distant, at least to Olena. The new queen hoped it would pass and eventually, it did. However, Zandria kept busy with her friends and the other queens kept Olena busy with lessons. This kept Zandria physically distant even after she apparently recovered emotionally.

As frustrated as she was with the constant teaching, Olena believed she needed the distraction. Otherwise, she would want to be running off with Zandria. She missed her sister and their time together. Olena missed Zandria more than she missed their mother. This made Olena feel a little guilty, but she never really knew her mother. Sometimes, when she was younger, Olena used to pretend Zandria was her mother. With Zandria gone so much these days, she truly felt lonely.

As Olena sat in front of Cinderella, that thought made her wish Zandria was here right now. She wanted to be back on their beach in

Banookanook, building a sand castle with her, instead of being taught how to hold a drinking glass.

Olena liked Cinderella, but she liked her etiquette lessons least of all the queens' lessons. Except, she did enjoy when the Queen of the Western Sun turned her attention to beauty lessons. Even at three-hundred-years-old, Olena believed Cinderella remained the most beautiful of the queens.

It made her laugh the day Cinderella decided to attempt to brush Olena's curly hair straight. Unlike Zandria or her mother's mostly straight hair, Olena always inexplicably had tight curls which she loved. The beautiful old woman fought with the bushy batch of curls for an hour before she accepted that Olena's curls were there to stay.

In another lesson, Cinderella taught her that it was impolite to ask a lady's age. However, Olena persisted until she got the answer of the queen's true age. She also learned that Isis was about one hundred years older and Snow White was the youngest at around two hundred years.

Olena's magic lessons with Isis also frustrated her recently. Not since the day she transported William to rescue Zandria in Peckwood Forest could she duplicate the Walking Portal. She understood how valuable it would be to be able to travel anywhere instantly. Yet, no matter how many times she touched her fingers together in a triangle pattern, the glowing portal would not appear.

Isis pressed her almost every day to keep trying. With each failed attempt, Olena wanted to try even less. She knew this affected her other abilities as well. She repeatedly failed Isis' other lessons. She knew the queens had hundreds of years of practice, but Olena struggled with the simplest of magical tasks. She even had to use her hand to open her bedroom door.

Luckily, Snow White did not act as demanding as the Queen of the Southern Valley. Each time Snow White returned from the Northern Wood, she would sit with Olena and simply tell her stories. Olena loved the musical sound of her voice, which did not seem affected by her two hundred or so years. The old woman still sounded like a young girl.

This day, the Queen of the Northern Wood began telling her about the history of the queens.

"Did you know you are only the fifth Queen of the Eastern Sky?" asked Snow White.

"I am?" Olena replied with a question.

"It's true," said Snow White. "In two thousand years, there have only been four eastern queens before you."

This thought impressed Olena. She said, "How do the queens live so long?"

"That is part of Castle Empyrean's Deep Magic," answered Snow White.

"Will I live for hundreds of years?"

Snow White paused for a moment. Olena thought she looked like she could not decide what to tell her.

Finally, Snow White said, "Remember, you were the youngest to ever become Queen of the Eastern Sky. Who knows? You may live to be older than us all."

Olena wanted to ask about Zandria or Kez. She wanted to know if the magic would work for her friends. She never saw any other old people with the other queens. She did not think they even had any friends. Olena decided not to ask because she was afraid the answer would be no. Despite being a queen, Olena still had the feelings of a child and did not want to think about losing her sister, now or in the future.

Snow White continued, "It is not quite time to tell of the First Queen, but that will be soon. For now, I want you to know that we are all the fifth in our succession."

"Suspension?" Olena tried to repeat the confusing word.

"No dear," chuckled Snow White. "Our succession. It means besides you, Cinderella, Isis and I are all the fifth in our lines to become a queen of one of the realms of Empyrean."

"Ka," said Olena. She used her universal Nookan word to express surprise. Cinderella frowned upon her using that word in polite company. It amused Olena that they each were number five. "Tell me about the other queens, please?"

"I wish we had time for more today," said Snow White. "I can't wait for you to learn about the Passing Queen."

"She's the last one that could do the Walking Portal like me," started Olena. Then she corrected herself, "I mean, like I did one time."

Olena could feel tears start to form at the corners of her eyes. She wished she could do it again.

"Do not fret, little one," comforted Snow White. "You will blossom into your true power soon enough. You should imagine that the Passing Queen had an even more difficult challenge in her time."

"Like what?" asked Olena.

"Well, all four queens mysteriously disappeared at the same time. Then this young girl appeared from nowhere. She saved Empyrean at one of its darkest moments, but only remained queen for a few days. That is why she is called the Passing Queen, because her time passed so quickly."

"She sounds amazing," said Olena, becoming perkier.

"She truly will be," answered Snow White. "She was also given that name because she surpassed everyone's expectations, like I think you will."

Olena enjoyed hearing of another young girl becoming queen. Then she noticed Snow White's words *will be*. That made it sound like the Passing Queen was in the future, instead of the past. Olena thought Snow White meant to say she *truly was*. Then she thought Snow White may succeed where Cinderella could not. She believed if she concentrated on the confusing statement too hard, it would stress her brain so much that her hair would uncurl.

Before Olena could ask about the word choice, Snow White continued, "The Passing Queen made way for the Thrice Queen. The Passing Queen belonged to all of Empyrean and not to any one land. That is why she is not counted in the succession. The Thrice Queen marked the calling of the third queen from each land at the same time."

"That is a lot of queens to remember," said Olena.

"You're right, but you have plenty of time to learn about them later," said Snow White. "Right now, I have a surprise for you, but I'll let your sister tell you about it."

"Zan? Zandria's here?" Olena jumped up and almost did not wait for one of the attending elves to lead her through the ever changing halls of Castle Empyrean.

After a few minutes of navigating the halls, the elf led Olena to Zandria's bedroom. Olena burst through the door to find Zandria sitting alone on the edge of her bed.

Zandria stood up as Olena rushed to her. They collided in a tremendous hug that toppled the sisters back onto the bed. Olena could barely hear Zandria's laughter over her own tears of joy.

After they regained their composure, Olena asked, "How long are you staying?"

"I'll be with you for a while," said Zandria. "That's part of the surprise."

"I know. Snow White told me." Olena could barely contain her excitement. She did not realize how much she actually missed Zandria.

"She told you the surprise?" said Zandria. She looked hurt.

"No," consoled Olena. "I mean she told me that you had a surprise."

Her big sister looked relieved.

Zandria said, "Good. I wanted to be the one to tell you that we are going home."

"Home?" Olena felt confusion overtake her excitement unexpectedly. She only recently started getting used to thinking of Castle Empyrean as home. She had not forgotten her life before becoming Queen of the Eastern Sky, but she thought of it in a different way now. She quickly realized what Zandria meant as her sister spoke.

Zandria clarified, "We're going to Banookanook, silly."

Olena tried to picture it in her head. She tried to remember the smooth sandy beach and the huts built partially out of those strange giant shells. The images stayed vague in her head. Then the memory of the werewolf attack overpowered her happier memories. All she could picture now was Kez leading them racing for their lives into the jungle.

She knew Banookanook was not really their home anymore. However, Olena did not care at this moment. She liked how happy Zandria looked and she loved the idea that they were going to do some travelling together. She did not care where they were going as long as they were going together. Being away from Castle Empyrean felt like an added bonus.

Apparently, Zandria had more to say, interrupting Olena's musings.

"Adam's horse friend, Kalis, told me the Palace by the Sea is crumbling. You're supposed to go to the east and rebuild it. You get to make your own sand castle."

This news excited Olena. She remembered living in sight of the Palace by the Sea. She remembered building small castles on the beach, pretending she was a princess and watching the waves wash them back into the sea. Now she would actually get to build her own castle.

Then Olena realized this would be the first time she stepped outside of Castle Empyrean in a year. She spent days watching Friesians pass through the gates or those miniature hawks flying out from the tallest towers. Many times, she wished she could soar with Captain Aeran as he flew off on his latest quest.

A knock came at the door. Zandria opened it to reveal Tym the elf. Olena noticed his hair braided exactly like Zandria's. She guessed this to be an elven hairstyle that Dew did for her sister.

Tym said, "If you have delivered the news, the others are almost done making preparations."

"We're leaving now?" asked Olena. It seemed unusual to be leaving so suddenly.

Tym smiled with affirmation, slightly revealing his pointed teeth.

"Let's go, baby sis," said Zandria. "I mean, Your Majesty." Zandria concluded with a giggle and a quick bow.

Tym led the sisters down to the courtyard. Olena could not believe what she saw there. So many people gathered like a surprise party. Adam and Dew waited by the Friesians, Kalis and Tihi. The Friesian General, Fury, stood harnessed to Snow White's carriage with another horse that Olena did not recognize. She watched her old quzzak friend Kez helping the wooden doll Sylvan up into the carriage. She wondered how many of her friends kept this surprise from her and for how long?

The driver of Snow White's carriage hopped down from his bench. Olena thought she remembered his name as Smoltz. After the Rockhorn Battle, the previous driver resigned his post to be with his family. This Smoltz had helped William free the slave children from the mines. Apparently, Snow White had honored him by making him her driver.

Smoltz ushered the girls into the carriage. As soon as Olena found a seat, Kez and Sylvan made their way to her lap.

A few moments later, the other three queens joined them. Olena sat comfortably between Zandria and Snow White. Isis and Cinderella sat opposite from them. Everyone acted as if they were going on a well-planned picnic. Olena could not say why this made her uncomfortable, but she felt strange all the same. She had been secluded in Castle Empyrean for a year for her own safety.

Now, all four queens were travelling across dangerous country together with very little protection.

Young Smoltz closed the door and climbed up to his seat. Then she heard Fury give his orders.

"Alright everybody, time to go," said the Friesian General.

Isis leaned toward Olena. She said, "Please, say the words."

Olena knew Isis meant for her to say the incantation to open the massive wall of thorns that protected Castle Empyrean's main gate. She whispered the words, but nothing happened.

Snow White patted Olena on the knee. "In its time, dear." Then she whispered the words and the briars rolled back like a lethal curtain allowing them to pass.

As they crossed the exquisite Vexwood bridge, it bothered Olena that her magic seemed to be getting worse instead of better. She felt terrible that she could not even leave the castle on her own if she wanted to. Still, she would not let it bring her down, having Zandria next to her made her too happy. Besides, they were going home. Olena listened to the sound of the wheels change as they left the fireproof wood and find their place in the ruts on the ancient dirt road.

Olena stared out the window at the expanse of tall grasses that made up the Central Plains. Fury and the other strong Friesian picked up speed as they turned east.

Chapter 3

Olena leaned across Zandria for the first part of the trip, staring out the window. Zandria did not seem to mind. Kez and Sylvan relocated to the floor of the spacious carriage in an effort to make everyone more comfortable. The gentle swaying of the ride seemed to put everyone at ease.

"I don't suppose we could do anything about the bumps?" asked Kez, revealing that he did not find the same comfort in the smoothness of the ride.

The seat cushions absorbed most of the shock for her and the other queens, but Olena could see her little friends being jolted quite a bit.

"Why don't you come back up here?" she offered.

"We wouldn't dream of it," squeaked Sylvan. Even though they took up very little space, the two small advisors did not want to make anyone unhappy.

It took a while for Olena to get used to Sylvan's high-pitched voice. It appeared to her that the other queens did not like it at all. Cinderella even put her fingers to her ears each time Sylvan spoke in her presence.

"Are you sure?" Olena asked.

"Absolutely," said Sylvan. The crooked smile she once painted on his little wooden head gave away no emotion. If he was unhappy about his situation, his permanently painted expression showed nothing but satisfaction.

Olena gave up sight-seeing after the second pirate ship passed them. She knew they preferred to be called traders these days. They even formed an official Trader's Guild with her old friend Mildoo Vol as its head. She liked Captain Vol and imagined he lead a very adventurous life, even as simple traders. Olena still liked to think of them as pirates. She thought that sounded much more exciting. She did not know much about the plains, though. Olena wondered with whom and to where they traded. There had to be villages or something somewhere out on the wide plains.

After another day of travel, the small party stopped for a brief rest near the western foothills of the Euphoric Mountains. Isis insisted they break now so as not to stop while under the effects of the mountains.

"They only make you happy," said Olena. She remembered walking through them once before.

"It can be much worse with a queen's magic," said Isis. "Even one with your limited abilities."

Olena did not think Isis meant to insult her. She tried not to be hurt by the words. Instead, she chose to concentrate on the words Snow White told her many times before when she felt this way. She believed her powers would come when it was time.

Although a slightly rougher ride, nothing happened to stop them amidst the mountains. Soon they were at the intersection of the Great Road and the Mountain Byway. There Olena saw something she almost forgot about.

This intersection had been turned into a supply post for the artisans and craftsmen working on the restoration of Soria Moria. Olena had promised the dilapidated castle to Zandria when she first became queen. Then shortly after that, her good friend William confirmed it had a troll infestation.

The Empyrical Wizards concocted a few potions to chase out the trolls. Following that, construction began. The original estimates said it would take four years to complete the restoration. Once the extent of the troll damage was discovered, they increased it to six years. With all the fuss, it made Olena happy to see work actually being done.

Eventually, Olena and Zandria ended up trading seats. Now into the Dead Forest, Olena wanted to watch out the window again.

"Ooh, there's another one." It thrilled Olena to see green leaves starting to sprout on the rotten trees.

About a year ago, William returned from the east with a special seed. He had somehow forgotten about his old life and his title of Prince during that journey. Olena decided not to talk about it because no one else seemed to notice the change. The way Zandria acted sometimes made her think that her sister also remembered finding William frozen. In a year's time, the girls had not had enough privacy to discuss it without anyone else, so it remained an unanswered question.

Aside from that, Olena remembered wanting to help fulfill William's wish of rebuilding the east. She cast the seed from one of Castle Empyrean's highest balconies. The magical seed disappeared over the eastern horizon in a blaze of light. She hoped it would restore this decimated land to the Royal Forest.

Finally, she had proof that it started. Of the hundreds of dead trees they passed between the Euphoric Mountains and the animal town of Bremen, Olena counted sixty green leaves.

In Bremen, the giant tiger, Virgata, greeted them with a party. Olena believed he had so far kept his promise as Mayor of Bremen. His animals turned Bremen back into a thriving town and an excellent place to spend the night before the long journey to Edge Town and the sea.

Virgata informed them that more travelers from as far away as Bond started using their town and the road east. He shared his opinion that they might be trying to rebuild some of the old villages.

"Only a month before," boasted the tiger, "we hosted a Trader's Guild ship."

"Pirates came across the mountains?" asked Zandria. Olena thought her sister sounded like she did not believe Virgata.

Virgata answered, "They had such a successful trip that they promised to come back next month."

"It must have been quite a sight to watch them roll out across the Wasteland," added Kez.

"Indeed," said Virgata. "With those winds, I'm sure they moved much faster than they expected."

The group spent the night in Bremen. Zandria stayed up late with her friends. This left Olena to go to bed early in her room at the boarding house. Tonight, she had her choice of rooms, but Virgata assured her that as she cared for the east, soon all of their rooms would always be full.

Kez and Sylvan shared Olena's room. She grew used to this at Castle Empyrean and had no intention of changing it. This furry quzzak and wooden doll had become her closest friends and most trusted advisors. Olena turned to them with any question without fear of sounding silly or insecure.

Sylvan had the experience of serving who knew how many years at the court in Soria Moria. His knowledge helped Olena pass more than a few tests. As the wise elder of his tribe, Kez could be counted on to help make difficult decisions.

Embarrassingly, Olena admitted that his acrobatics and stunts also made her laugh.

At the moment, Kez balanced on the narrow bedpost. He looked preoccupied, picking at his tail.

"I'm nervous," confessed Olena to her two confidants. She did not know if she wanted to say anything.

"About what?" asked Kez.

"The queens are expecting me to rebuild the Palace by the Sea. I don't think I have the power to do that." Olena felt a little better by telling her feelings to her friends.

"They would not bring you all this way if they did not believe in you," said Sylvan.

Olena said, "Besides, I'm not sure I want to live there. I never really liked it. Zandria always wanted to live in the palace. I was happy with our hut."

"But the hut has a sand floor," said Kez.

"What?" snickered Olena.

Kez explained, "I have to say I have grown accustomed to a solid, clean floor beneath my paws. I know that is no way for a creature of the jungle to speak, but there it is."

Olena laughed hard now. She said, "Kez, you're spoiled."

"A life of privilege can easily lead to a life of laziness," offered Sylvan. "My suggestion would be to tell the other queens how you feel and then decide what is best for you."

She liked the sound of that idea, but did not know if she would have the courage to speak her mind to the other queens.

"I at least want to see Banookanook first. I barely remember it," Olena said. Then she blew out the candle and quickly fell asleep.

The kind animals of Bremen bid the queens farewell the next morning. The four Friesians carried their passengers, two with saddle and two with carriage, off into the Wasteland.

Olena saw very little outside, but she was now stuck with the window seat. Zandria stated she did not want to trade back. The queens did not speak much. Olena guessed they did not want to talk in front of Zandria. Cinderella told her once that many things they had to say were only meant for queen's ears. Their positions forbid them from certain topics in front of others.

Olena passed the time trying to count sinkholes. She knew what they represented and knew most of them went far underground. That did not stop her need for something to eliminate the tedium.

Then she yelled, "Stop!"

Zandria pulled out her dagger, apparently on instinct. She looked ready for danger.

"Please stop the carriage," Olena said again.

This time, she heard Smoltz signal to Fury. The carriage came to a rough stop. Zandria tried to stop Olena as she jumped from the halted carriage.

"What is it?" she heard Zandria say from right behind her. It made Olena feel good to know that

Zandria still wanted to protect her. The three other queens waited in the carriage.

Olena stepped over a narrow crack and knelt down on the ashy gray dirt. She looked in amazement at a tiny sapling struggling to live.

"Is that a tree?" asked Zandria.

"Hopefully it will be," said Olena.

Kez approached, "I expected the Dead Forest to eventually be revived, but this is awesome."

"I never guessed the Wasteland could be restored," said Olena.

"That's great news," added Fury from the road.

Snow White stepped out of the carriage as the girls returned.

She said, "You realize that you did this?"

"I did?" said Olena.

"You should never doubt your abilities," said Snow White. "You planted the seed that will someday return the Royal Forest to all of this forsaken land."

Olena spent the rest of the ride through the Wasteland trying to imagine what it would look like covered with trees. She hoped new towns could even be built on the revived land. For now, she saw no other trees.

Eventually, they crossed the Wasteland and she did see some other trees. The party entered the coastal jungle and a familiar sense came over Olena. She truly had forgotten the look of her old home. The tall palm trees seemed strange to her.

Close to the end of the Great Road, Olena thought she spotted someone staring at her, hidden in the bushes. A pair of fierce eyes locked with hers for an instant and then was gone. Could it be a dwarf or a Nookan, she wondered? Whoever it was did not run away, the eyes simply vanished. Olena concluded it was her imagination due to her anxiousness.

As they entered the Edge Town market, the anxious feeling did not ease. The light skinned Easterners that Olena travelled with seemed more normal to her now than the Nookans she grew up with. She honestly did not recall the Nookans having such dark skin.

Fury brought the carriage to a stop at what used to be the front gate of the Palace by the Sea.

"Everybody out, end of the line," he joked.

When Olena took her turn to get out of the carriage, she saw Adam and Dew already exploring the ruins. It made Olena sad to see what amounted to nothing more than some big piles of sand with a gaping chasm in the middle. She guessed that hole to be the way Adam escaped from the Rockhorn mines underground.

Olena tried to picture the old palace. She could almost make out the remains of its high curved walls and beautiful spiral columns. Now, almost nothing remained.

Then Isis made her way to the edge of the chasm, leaning on her sistrum-cane for support. She looked down into the abyss.

"There is no magic here," she said, definitively.

"Our old friend is completely gone," added Cinderella.

Isis began waving her hand in a circular motion with her palm facing the open maw. As she did, she mumbled something that Olena could not hear. With the circular motion, dirt and dust began to swirl around the edges.

Adam must have wanted a better view and moved up next to Isis. Olena knew this hole was important to him. She watched his face as he watched chunks of rock break loose from the steep walls.

Isis continued to wave her arm. More rocks and sand swirled into the mix. The piles of sand that used to be the palace walls slid between their feet and from the other sides as they were sucked into the hole. Soon, the entire crevasse became a whirling mass of rock and sand.

Olena had to cover her ears to block out the roar of the debris. It reminded her of a storm. Then as abruptly as Isis started, she stopped waving her hand. The sandstorm stopped and instantly sealed the chasm.

Looking around, Olena saw only vacant ground. Nothing remained to prove that the hole or Palace by the Sea ever existed.

"Now it is your turn," Isis said to Olena.

"Turn for what?" asked Olena. She could guess what Isis meant. She did not want this moment to be here already.

Cinderella said, "It's your turn to create a Palace by the Sea. Your predecessor willed her palace into existence with only her heart and mind. You must do the same on this very spot."

Olena guessed correctly. The queens wanted her to use magic to build a new palace. They insisted the last Queen of the Eastern Sky did it, although she thought she remembered childhood stories to the contrary. In the version she heard, eastern craftsmen and Nookans built the palace. Olena looked to Kez and Sylvan for support. They were nowhere to be seen.

"But," began Olena. The she started to cry. She could not contain herself any longer.

Zandria and Dew ran over to comfort her. Olena liked Zandria's elven friend. She always seemed so confident.

"What is it, Olena?" asked Snow White.

"I can't do it," she blurted and then ran down the beach.

Olena left the others behind and quickly found herself tumbling down the rocky slope that marked the edge of Banookanook. She could barely tell where she was through her tears. Luckily, she did not hurt herself on the dull red and brown rocks.

Her dress snagged on one of the rocks and she tripped. Before Olena got back up, she kicked off her shoes. Suddenly, she felt transported. The soft, warm sand pressed between her small toes. She remembered learning how to walk for the first time on this sand. She knew Banookanook truly was her home. It felt good to be home.

By the time she made it among the huts, Olena completely stopped crying. The Nookans did not pay her much attention. They looked busy with their boats and nets. She guessed fishing season had to be at its peak and the colorful regins were not going to jump out of the water on their own. She used to spend hours watching the red, yellow and blue fish do their underwater dance. Then a tinge of sadness struck her as she remembered the day Aeran came to warn the eastern queen. He tried to catch a regin even though they were bigger than him. It made her sad because of all the other memories that came from that fateful day.

Olena forced her mind to happier thoughts. She liked to feel at home. For six years, this place made her feel happy and safe. The troubles of a young queen seemed very far away. She made a decision at that moment.

Zandria caught up to her first, followed closely by Dew and Adam.

"Are you okay?" asked Zandria.

"Happier than I've been in a year, Zan."

It took a little longer for Smoltz to help the three older queens down onto the beach. Finally, they confronted Olena.

"What is the meaning of this?" demanded Isis.

Snow White said, "I think I understand. I was alone and scared once. Things will be fine."

Olena summoned up her courage and told her feelings to the queens. She said, "I don't want to be like the last Queen of the Eastern Sky. I want to be myself. I made a decision to build my castle here, in Banookanook."

One of the nearby Nookan fishermen took an interest in Olena's words.

Dew interrupted, "You can't destroy these people's homes to build yours."

"I didn't mean right here," explained Olena. "I meant over there, so it's still a part of Banookanook." She pointed out at the water.

Dew and Adam laughed at the plan. Olena had no intention of being funny and she gave them a look that hopefully conveyed that. Their laughs quickly died down to a few small giggles.

"You mean on the water? Like a floating castle?" asked Cinderella. "But how?"

Now the Nookan fisherman stood. "Pardon me, Your Majesties. I recognize her as a child of our village and as the Queen of the Eastern Sky. If she wants a floating palace, we will build it for her."

Olena hugged the fisherman, although she did not even know his name. For an instant, his muscular body reminded her of her father. The pain of losing her father seeped back into her mind. Then the sadness quickly turned into excitement as the other queens agreed.

"What do you want to call your new home?" asked Snow White.

"I'll call it the Palace on the Sea."

Chapter 4

Kez did not see when Olena ran off or hear her proclamation. He had his own reasons for coming back to Banookanook.

As soon as the carriage stopped, Kez sprang out the open window. He grabbed the top of the frame and flipped upward, doing a complete back flip and landing on his feet on top of the carriage. Sometimes, at his age, he even impressed himself with his agility. From here, he could see the ruins of the palace, the beach and the jungle.

The jungle.

Kez did not realize how much he missed it until he saw it again. Only a few nights ago, he slept on a thick mattress with warm blankets. He almost forgot his first home and everything he left behind. He knew he wanted to see his family. He figured he had grandchildren by now that he had never met. This past year, living in luxury, he almost forgot about living in the wild. He felt embarrassed by his comments back at Bremen. He instantly discovered he actually missed things like sleeping outside in a gentle rain.

The quzzak shimmied down the side of the carriage and started for the jungle while the others looked into the giant hole.

"Excuse me." Sylvan's high-pitched voice stopped Kez in his tracks. "Where might you be going?"

Kez did not want to lie to the wooden man. They had become quite good friends over the past year. They found a common bond in that the bigger people tended to overlook them.

"I had an urge to see my old home," explained Kez. He did not know if Sylvan would understand the emotional reasons for that.

"I see," said Sylvan. "Very instinctive of you."

The quzzak answered, "As they say, you can take the animal out of the jungle, but not the other way around."

"You are not too spoiled then?" said Sylvan. He referred to their earlier discussion.

"Not so spoiled that I don't enjoy the sun warming my fur or napping in an afternoon breeze." Kez realized he missed the jungle more than he previously let himself believe.

Kez moved toward the jungle again.

"May I?" called Sylvan.

"May you come with me?" replied Kez.

Sylvan stood silent. Kez could not guess what he was thinking because his crudely painted expression never changed. He knew Olena wanted to make Sylvan more human, but she did not have a very steady hand when it came to art. The child's version of a face on Sylvan's smooth round head almost made Kez feel sorry for him.

"Of course, my friend," said Kez.

They disappeared into the jungle at the same time Isis sealed the chasm.

Sylvan's little round head kept spinning in every direction. Kez deduced Sylvan had never been in a place like this. He must either be very impressed or very frightened as he tried to take in his new surroundings.

When they were completely out of sight of their traveling companions, Kez gave a quzzak shriek. As the elder of his clan, he knew that his yell would summon all quzzaks that heard it.

Soon, the trees seemed to come alive. Unmoving jungle vegetation a moment ago, now the branches swarmed with quzzaks. Males, females and babies scurried down from the dense canopy. Kez saw fur of brown, tan and black dashing about. Very few had his distinguished gray colored coat.

The quzzaks welcomed Kez and his strange friend with hospitality and excitement. Kez embraced his family members, old and new. Before long, they sat among the high palms. Kez ate his fill of tropical fruit while Sylvan told stories of their adventures. Normally, this job belonged to Kez. The quzzaks called him the Storykeeper for good reason. Today, however, Kez did not mind letting his wooden friend share their stories.

Sylvan recounted the Rockhorn battle and the encounter with Evorin the dragon. He told of the pirate Mildoo Vol and how the animals of Bremen joined the battle. The idea of a town run only by animals intrigued the quzzaks. Some said they would love to see this town. Sylvan told as much as he knew about the Trammeler and Raymond Shaydaway too. A few of the older quzzaks remembered Zandria and Olena's mother. They remembered her being a kind and loving woman. They said she was friend to both quzzak and Nookan. They missed her, but found relief that she had been saved.

While Kez listened to the stories of the girls and their friends, he wished for something more. He never thought of himself as the adventurous type, but now he found himself wanting his own adventure. He secretly hoped that he might find his own quest. Maybe, he thought, he and Sylvan could go on their own journey. Then he thought about how slow Sylvan's little body moved and realized he would not make a very good partner if they were in a hurry for any reason.

Maybe, he was not destined for anything greater than to be Olena's friend. In his heart, Kez was fine with that.

After staying up most of the night, Kez slept for a short while. His private hope of becoming a hero faded into peaceful dreams. He knew neither him nor Sylvan would ever have to worry about having their own adventure. He planned to live safely in the castle with no chance of being in danger in a strange land or anything like that.

As morning came, Kez reluctantly gave his goodbyes. He had a tinge of regret leaving them behind. But the quzzaks did not meddle in human affairs and Kez knew Olena needed him more than they did. He and Sylvan made it back to the carriage in time for them to leave. Hundreds of quzzaks joined the Nookans and Edge Towners to say bye and wish them a safe journey.

Chapter 5

The rhythmic sound of the waves comforted Olena in her sleep. She did not realize it, but the waves matched the sound of her mother's heartbeat before Olena was born. The repetitive thump and whoosh of the moving water somehow reassured her that she was safe.

Olena woke up feeling refreshed. Despite her recent frustrations with magic, she felt everything would be fine. The peace she gained from sleeping by the ocean made her feel better. She did not want to test her magic today, but any lack of it now seemed less stressful. She looked forward to sleeping by the ocean every night once her castle was done.

Some final discussions left the Nookans with an immense task. Without the use of magic, they planned to build a fortified, floating palace. The inhabitants of Banookanook definitely understood the sea. They promised the palace would be anchored in the best spot to minimize rocking or drifting and still be clear of the fishing lanes.

They finished the meeting with turtle egg omelets and fresh pineapple juice from the jungle. Then all of the Nookans and people of Edge Town came out to bid them farewell. It surprised Olena to see hundreds of quzzaks follow Kez and Sylvan out of the jungle. She knew there were other quzzaks, but did not guess there were so many of the furry little creatures. They chittered and jumped up and down. It made Olena laugh. She wished she could take them all back to Castle Empyrean. Then she promised herself the Palace on the Sea would always be open to everyone, but especially quzzaks.

Fury and his Friesians made good time across the Wasteland. The queens said very little on the way back to Bremen. Olena guessed they were satisfied with the outcome of the trip.

In Bremen, Virgata greeted them with his usual courtesy. Olena liked the animal town much more now than her first experience, back when they planned to eat her. Still, she did not find the same satisfaction sleeping in the forest town that she felt sleeping on the beach.

The party left early the next morning. So early, that Olena dozed as the carriage rolled along the Great Road. She drifted between awake and asleep which is why she thought she dreamt the creature moving through the trees of the Dead Forest.

At first, she only caught glimpses, fighting against her heavy eyelids. It seemed something white followed alongside them. Whatever it was, it kept its distance off the Great Road. The figure held Olena's attention as she gradually shook off sleep. The thing moved quickly despite the tangled undergrowth. Olena remembered the thick brambles made it difficult to walk through the Dead Forest.

Finally, Olena sat up, wide awake. She watched intently as the white shape flashed between the trees.

Zandria must have noticed her change in seating and asked, "What's so interesting?"

"Something's following us," said Olena, pointing out the southern facing window of the carriage.

Zandria leaned over her shoulder.

"I don't see anything," she said.

With that, whatever had been following them burst from the undergrowth and leapt across the road in front of them.

Fury and the other Friesian rapidly stopped the carriage. Kez and Sylvan tumbled off of Olena's lap. Olena jumped up to look out the opposite window. She could see nothing.

"Stay back," warned Zandria. "It might be dangerous."

Olena looked at her sister to acknowledge her concern. Then she noticed a black shape through the window behind Zandria. Olena realized they were now surrounded. The white creature remained out of sight on the north side of the road and now a black creature moved in from the south. Adam urged Kalis up from behind the carriage into a defensive position. Dew and Tihi took the other side.

The young queen looked to her elders for guidance. Cinderella and Isis both looked concerned, but Snow White had a slight smile.

"What's so funny?" asked Olena.

"I do not think we are in any danger," said Snow White.

Then from outside, Fury shouted, "I know that scent."

Snow White offered her hand to Zandria for help up from the cushioned bench. She leaned out the window and gently said, "Please, come out now."

After a moment, a beautiful white unicorn emerged from the forest. Her golden horn glistened as the morning sun finally climbed over the Euphoric Mountains off to the west. Then Olena sprang to the other side of the carriage as the black creature stepped onto the road. She immediately recognized the old black war horse.

Before she could say his name, Fury exclaimed, "Wrath!"

Olena barely knew the Friesian, but she remembered he led their army against the Rockhorns. After that, Wrath left with Sayonya, the leader of the unicorn. She thought they now lived in the Unicorn Meadow somewhere south of Bremen.

All of the passengers unloaded from the carriage to greet the horse and unicorn.

Wrath explained, "We heard the queens were coming east. News travels fast now that the forest is starting to live again."

"We've seen proof of that along the road," said Olena.

"Then I wish you could see our meadow," said Sayonya. "Flowers are blooming that I haven't seen for a hundred years, plus there are some new ones that I don't even recognize. Everything is so beautiful there."

Then Zandria stepped up to Wrath. Olena thought she looked embarrassed.

"Excuse me," said Zandria.

"Yes, child," answered Wrath.

"I wanted to say thank you for helping me and Adam last year. I never felt like I said it properly and worried that I'd never get the chance."

Wrath looked humbled. He lowered his head and said, "It was my honor."

Adam added, "That goes for me too."

Wrath raised his head and stuck out his chest in what Fury called his military pose. Then he addressed the Friesians.

"I understand you are all doing me proud."

"It's no easy task," said Fury.

"But we do our best," added Kalis.

Tihi said, "You have left us large horseshoes to fill."

Olena enjoyed watching the old friends converse. Then she smiled with Fury's expression that looked like a cross between forgetfulness and surprise. He must have thought Wrath did not know Tihi, she guessed.

"Oh," said Fury. "Tihi can talk."

"You seem surprised," said Wrath.

"But she never did before. Am I the only one that didn't know?" said Fury.

Wrath said, "The Silent Tihi has the wisdom to know when not to speak. Besides, with you in charge, who could ever get a word in?"

Everyone laughed at Fury's expense. He faked being indignant.

"Seriously though," said Wrath, "being a general suits you. You have become an excellent representative of our kind."

Now Fury looked embarrassed. "It's only because I had such a great teacher."

"We all did," added Tihi.

"He is still a great leader," said Sayonya.

Olena noticed how Sayonya and the Friesians looked at Wrath. She even thought the queens showed him great respect. He led the Friesian army during one of the longest times of peace in Empyrean's history according to Snow White. However, his training and diligence prepared them for the Rockhorn

Battle. If not for his training, Olena believed, the Forgotten Evil may have won that day and she would never have become queen.

"We do not mean to delay your travels any longer," said Wrath. "We simply wanted the brief company of old friends and to share our news."

"What news is that, noble Wrath?" asked Snow White.

"I'll let Sayonya tell it."

The unicorn explained, "For some time, hunting of our kind has been increasing. Although we do not possess the magic we once did, we are still being captured or worse for our horns. Even in our meadow, we are no longer safe." She paused, then addressed Zandria, "Thanks to you, at least one of our herd has been returned. You should know, Cayomi, who you rescued from that evil carnival, is healing well. Sadly, I do not believe her horn will ever grow back."

Zandria did look saddened by that news. Olena remembered her sister talking of the unicorn that Raymond Shaydaway tortured. Zandria kept her promise to save Cayomi and then the unicorn helped stop Shaydaway and end his plans to capture the queens in the crystal Trammeler. It made Olena happy to know the unicorn found her way back to her kind.

"How will you protect yourself?" asked Dew.

"Wrath and I have decided to lead the herd to the far east. Beyond the Great Cliffs, near the sea is supposed to be a land where we can remain hidden and free."

Olena thought about her history lessons for a moment. She recalled that both unicorns and dragons used to roam all of Empyrean by the thousands. Over time, their numbers diminished. She wondered if that meant Empyrean's magic was shrinking too.

She knew that unicorns, like the queens, were connected to the Deep Magic, but did not know much about where it came from or what would happen if it went away. Olena wished she knew more about the creation of Empyrean. Maybe with the Forgotten Evil trying to return and magical creatures like the unicorns leaving, Olena thought they might be coming into troubled times.

After that, a few more words were said about the safety of all of Empyrean's citizens. The three elder queens expressed their confidence that things would be fine. Whether they believed it or not, the older ladies said things would be more peaceful now, as it had been almost a year without any major troubles.

Olena shared a look with Zandria that meant their experiences may prove otherwise. Olena guessed Zandria felt the same as her. She felt that things would be getting worse before better. The queens did not seem to want to dwell on the subject and quickly boarded the carriage.

The Friesians bid their farewells. Before Olena realized it, they were on their way again. Fury and Wrath's last words rang in her ears.

"Will I ever see you again, old nag?" asked the younger Friesian.

"Only time will tell," answered the older horse.

For the rest of the trip back to Castle Empyrean, Olena thought about the unicorns. She admired their freedom. She wished she did not have to be trapped in the castle all the time, constantly under watch.

The queens did not want to talk about the growing danger across their lands, but they treated Olena like she was always in danger. Olena felt she needed time alone. She knew she had responsibility to her throne, but she wanted to be a kid. She wanted to play on the beach with her sister or maybe explore new places like Zandria did.

Instead, she felt stuck.

Chapter 6

𓄿𓄿𓄿 𓂋𓄿𓄿𓂝𓄿

Back at the castle, everything returned to normal. Almost everything.

Olena had her usual lessons with Snow White and Cinderella. When it came time for her magic lessons, Isis took Olena to one of the high balconies looking out over the plains toward the south.

Today, Isis looked old. Olena knew she had lived several hundred years longer than normal southerners and she always had silver hair and wrinkles. However, something seemed different. The Queen of the Southern Valley did not have her normal energy or intensity.

"Do you see that?" Isis pointed a crooked finger far below.

Olena could see the wall of thorns that protected this side of the castle. Slightly to the west of that she could see where the bottomless canyon widened. She thought Isis pointed at the canyon wall.

"I can't see anything," said Olena.

Isis sighed. "That is the problem. Once there was a mighty river that flowed all the way from my land to make a beautiful waterfall here."

Olena looked again. This time, some of her magic must have worked on its own. It felt like her eyes zoomed out of her head and suddenly she seemed to be standing on the edge of the canyon. The effect lasted only an instant, but she had time to see the tiniest trickle of water that inched a small stream across the plains to fall in drips over the canyon edge. Then the magic stopped and Olena found she never left the safety of the balcony. Without trying, she had discovered a new power.

"I saw it," she said.

Isis continued, "It's called Brygos or the River of Life by my people. Once, it flowed from the far south and even met with the Chromisarc in the east and the Scarbeck in the west. It used to be the greatest of all of Empyrean's rivers. Several hundred years ago, the people of the far south restricted its flow."

Olena wondered about the far south. "What people?"

"They live beyond Empyrean's borders," answered Isis. "We do not even have a name for them or know what they look like." This felt like an untruth to Olena, but she did not say so.

Olena could not believe it. She did not even know all of the people of Empyrean. Now Isis tells her there are people beyond their borders. That meant Empyrean actually had an end. More than the far south, Olena tried to imagine if someplace existed beyond the sea by Banookanook.

Isis interrupted Olena's thoughts. "After so long, these people are now raising a dispute over our border. They insist that some farmers have expanded their meager crops onto their land."

Olena did not understand why crossing borders could cause such trouble.

"There are talks from their ambassador of possible hostilities against us if the borders are not redrawn. Still, our maps indicate we have not crossed any boundaries. We don't even have farms near the border."

Olena said, "They're only lines on paper, they don't mean anything."

"Those lines are very important to some people. Also, they may be using it as an excuse to hide their true purpose. That is why I have to put our lessons on hold for a while. I have to return to the Infinity Temple in Hierakonpolis."

Olena knew the city of Hierakonpolis was the capital of the Southern Valley thanks to her tedious lessons with Snow White. Finally, the geography lessons seemed to be worth it. A year ago, Olena only knew the sands of Banookanook. Now she knew places all across

Empyrean. At least she did not feel completely lost when talking about the other queens' homes. Also, Olena learned that the Queen of the Southern Valley lived in the Infinity Temple when not at Castle Empyrean.

Olena felt disappointed and relieved at the same time. She did not want any of the queens to have difficulties. It seemed to be another sign that things were not all right in Empyrean. Still, she felt relieved to stop the annoying magic lessons for now.

In a surprising show of emotion, Isis hugged Olena. Then the old queen said, "I leave for the Southern Valley in the morning."

Chapter 7

Isis' sudden departure left Olena feeling confused. All she thought about for so long was being free of her lessons. She could not stand doing the same thing every day. Seeing Sayonya and thinking about the other unicorns only made her want freedom more.

Now that Isis had gone south, the other queens stopped their lessons too. Olena had some of the freedom she wanted, but still was not allowed to leave Castle Empyrean.

Her frustration with her magic abilities turned into boredom. She spent two days in her room with only Kez and Sylvan for company. Zandria, Dew and Adam left for Truewood Forest again. In the past several months, Zandria could barely sit still. Among other things, Dew had been teaching Zandria how to use a bow and arrow.

Zandria decided she liked practicing with the other elves. So this time, they headed north to try her archery skills with the rest of Dew's clan.

This left Olena to entertain herself. First, she tried on every dress in her closet, over one hundred. Most fit her perfectly, but some were too big, too small, too tight or too loose. She loved the blue silk, the purple velvet and red satin. Some of the softest cotton came from the Southern Valley.

That brought her thoughts back to Queen Isis. Olena had only been from Banookanook to Castle Empyrean. She listened to the queens and others talk about all of the amazing places across Empyrean. She tried to picture them in her head. Every place sounded so wonderful. She wished she could visit them all, or at least one. Any place had to be better than sitting in her bedroom, she thought.

Maybe she could go to the Southern Valley? At least there would be another queen there, so it would not be like she was unsupervised, Olena reasoned.

Olena did not discuss it with Kez or even think about asking permission. Sitting in a pile of dresses on her bed, she raised her hands, palms outward.

Kez must have realized what she was doing. He said, "Where are you trying to go?"

"Away," said Olena as she touched her thumbs together to form a triangle with her hands.

Nothing happened.

"Ugh," growled Olena. She flopped back on the bed and stared at the ceiling. It really made her unhappy that not even her Walking Portal would work.

After a moment, two faces appeared in her vision, blocking her view of the reflective ceiling. Kez leaned in from the left and Sylvan from the right.

"You weren't going to go somewhere without us, were you?" asked Kez.

As Olena sat up, Kez leapt to the headboard. She said, "I don't know."

Sylvan added, "I don't think she was going anywhere. Not with the state of her magic."

Olena knew he was being honest, but she did not like it. She shoved a pile of clothes on top of the little wooden man. The sudden movement caused Olena to lose her own balance and she tumbled to the floor.

"Help! Get me out!" came a muffled squeal from Sylvan.

Instantly, Olena felt bad for burying her friend. Before she could get up, Kez already rescued Sylvan. Then Kez gave Olena a disappointed look. This made Olena want to leave the room. She turned toward the door and tripped on another pile of clothes. The random mess padded her fall. She let herself lay face first on the floor, more emotionally hurt than physically. She started crying.

Despite her behavior, both Kez and Sylvan came over to comfort her.

"You Majesty," said Sylvan, "We didn't realize."

Kez said, "I know this has been difficult for you, but we did not guess you were so unhappy."

"I only want to be a kid," exclaimed Olena. She wanted to play in the sand and not have any responsibilities. Kids were not supposed to be responsible. That job belonged to parents. This made her think about her own parents. She held back her tears. Olena felt like her life had changed too much. Besides, how could she miss something she never really had? Realizing now how much Kez and Sylvan cared for her made her feel a little better.

"I'm sorry to have to say that time has passed," said Kez. "None of us get to be what we used to be."

"But Zandria gets to do whatever she wants," said Olena.

Sylvan responded, "Your sister is not the Queen of the Eastern Sky."

"It's not fair," whined Olena. "The other queens go where they please."

"The other queens have spent the last year with you. Their only goal has been helping and teaching you," said Kez.

Olena sat up, now calmer. She said, "Why does Isis get to go home?"

"The Queen of the Southern Valley was called away on urgent business," said Sylvan.

"Besides," said Kez, "we were in Banookanook only a few days ago."

Olena knew he was right. She felt a little foolish and maybe she was being selfish. It did not make her any less unhappy though.

Kez explained, "I miss our days on the beach too. Playing in the sand was definitely more fun than history lessons. However, things have changed. You are part of something bigger now. Whatever power created the Deep Magic of Empyrean planned this for you a millennia before you were born. It may not be what you want or like, but you are Queen of the Eastern Sky for a purpose."

Olena had not thought about it like that before. At seven years old, she never thought about her purpose or any greater plan.

Then Sylvan squeaked, "And you are the youngest queen ever for a reason as well. I do not know why, but I do know my history. From what I've seen in the past year, you may yet become the greatest Queen of the Eastern Sky as well."

Olena did not know if she wanted that, but she appreciated the kind words. She understood being a queen came with a great responsibility. If Empyrean wanted her, then she guessed Empyrean would give her the abilities she needed to be queen when the time was right. Whatever larger plan she might be a part of, Olena knew she was where she was supposed to be.

"Now, how about we clean this room of yours," suggested Kez.

As with any child, it took far longer to clean the mess than it took to make it. Olena hung up dress after dress while Kez and Sylvan folded and sorted. As she worked through the piles, she wrestled with her frustrations. Despite feeling like a part of something greater, she could not suppress her desire to have the same abilities as the other queens. For now, Olena tried to put it out of her head.

Eventually, Olena only had a few neatly arranged piles that needed to be tucked into drawers. When she opened the last drawer, she saw some things she had almost forgotten.

In what felt like another life, she met the rainbow fairies under a waterfall. The gifts they gave her now rested in this drawer, unneeded for so long. She saw the hand mirror that reflected only the truth. She remembered using it to help free William from his icy prison, even if no one else did. She also managed to save a leaf from Ruby's mayflower that flew her across the canyon and into Castle Empyrean for the first time. Now the large petal looked faded and brittle.

Then in the back corner of the drawer, Olena noticed the light reflect off one more thing. She reached in and pulled out a small bronze ring. Olena had a recollection of Ultramarine, the blue rainbow princess, giving it to her.

She could remember the fairy saying, "Some things are not as they look. What is hidden inside is often more valuable than the appearance on the outside."

At the time, Olena thought Ultramarine meant that there might be something inside the ring. Now with everything else, she guessed the blue fairy meant what was inside her. Although she was only a child, Empyrean decided to make her a queen.

Olena held the ring up for Kez and Sylvan to see. It looked as if the strip of metal had been pounded flat and polished before being bent into its crescent moon shape. While she looked, Olena remembered seeing a face reflected on the inner surface. At least, she thought she saw that the first time. She had looked several times after and even now saw nothing.

Then she said to her friends, "You know." She clicked her tongue against her teeth as she usually did when she wanted to say something important. "I never did try this thing on."

Olena slipped the ring on her thumb because it was too big for any of her other fingers.

The room suddenly turned upside down, but Olena did not feel anything move. Then the room turned again and again, faster and faster. Everything spun out of control. Olena shut her eyes. When she opened them, the room kept spinning, top to bottom. Olena wanted to move, but it scared her. Finally, she took a step backward and as quickly as the spinning started, it stopped.

However, she no longer stood in her bedroom.

Instead of the bright crystal walls of her room, Olena saw only dark, metallic walls. Somehow, she had been transported to a dark hallway. She looked closer and saw the walls, floor and low ceiling were made of the same bronze as the ring still on her left thumb.

She looked ahead and the hallway continued as far as she could see. Behind her, she saw what looked like a mirror in an ornate bronze frame. However, it did not reflect her image. Instead, she could see through it like a window.

Through the smoky glass, Olena could make out her bedroom. Kez and Sylvan looked like they were frantically searching for something. It must be her, Olena thought. She guessed from their point of view, she must have disappeared.

Olena pushed against the mirror, hoping to go through it back to her room. She only felt the cold glass. She pounded on it, but apparently Kez and Sylvan could not hear her. Now, Olena started to panic. Wherever she was, she was trapped.

Olena turned back to what was a long hallway a moment ago. Maybe, she thought, she could find a way out on the other end. Instead of the unending hall, she now found herself in a large square room. Everything still looked bronze, including the three statues now in the middle of the room.

The three figures looked strangely alive, but did not move. Olena forgot her initial panic of being trapped and walked closer to the figures. She inspected each statue with fascination.

Someone had arranged them in a triangle pattern. The one in the front center looked like a young girl. Olena guessed her to be close to Zandria's age. She had the facial features that Olena recognized in Isis, William's friend Aleta and other southern women she had met. She had that same strong, intense look. The metal did not do it justice, but Olena thought the real girl that inspired this statue must have had beautiful curly hair much like her own.

The second figure to the left could have been a woman. Olena guessed it to be a woman because she was tall and thin, but otherwise looked quite mysterious. She could not be completely sure of the gender because the head was covered with some type of turban. Only her eyes showed. She wore a tight shirt that did not reveal anything and tight pants wrapped into the top of her long boots. Elbow length gloves covered her hands and slender fingers.

Olena turned to the last statue. She looked at an enormous man, not quite as wide as he was tall, but shorter than the previous figure. Even in bronze form, he looked friendly with round cheeks, a thick moustache and a bald head.

A strange feeling came over Olena, like she was being watched. She looked back at the tall figure. A moment ago, the statue faced forward. Even though the room was dim, Olena knew she faced forward. Now the woman looked directly at her. Olena turned back to the man. Where both his eyes were open when she first saw him, one was now squinted closed in a perpetual wink.

Panic started to return. Olena did not see these statues move, but they changed positions. She could not understand it and did not like it. She took a step back in order to see both the tall woman and big man statues. She only blinked for a second and when she opened her eyes, both statues leaned in, frozen and facing directly at her.

Olena took another step back, not wanting to look away again. This time, she bumped into something. Her heart raced as she turned around.

"Boo," said the bronze girl.

Olena screamed, "Ka!"

The young girl stepped down off her square pedestal and stood face to face with Olena. After scaring her, the girl started to giggle. Olena did not think it was funny to scare anyone like that. She stumbled backwards. The skinny woman stepped behind her, putting both hands on her shoulders to keep her from moving.

Olena felt scared and trapped. Right now, she would trade anything to be sitting for one of Cinderella's etiquette lessons. If only she could use magic to protect herself, she wished.

Then the large man hoisted himself from the chair that was hidden by his girth. He stepped down from his pedestal.

"Now doan be scarit, liddel lady," he said with an unusual accent. How could he tell her to not be scared, pondered Olena. Of course she was scared. She found herself trapped in a room with three statues that came to life. Olena believed this would be enough to scare anyone.

As he spoke, Olena could see past his metal teeth, and inside his head. She discovered he was hollow. Unlike the mighty Eisenhahn whose skin turned to iron, these were not people covered in bronze, but actual statues come to life.

She tried not to be scared, but Olena did not know if these beings wanted to hurt her.

"Aw, she's trembling," said the girl. At first, she appeared genuinely concerned, but then her smile told Olena she was teasing.

"Stop it, Ovara," said the big man.

The girl did stop. She turned to the man and asked, "What's my name?"

He repeated, almost like he was not sure, "Ovara?"

Ovara shrugged. She said, "Good enough, I guess. What's your name this time?"

The man looked to be thinking, trying to remember his name. Finally, he said, "Ogustus."

"What about that one?" said Ovara, pointing at the skinny woman still standing silently behind Olena.

"She must be Omarika," said Ogustus. "Which means your name must begin witz an O," he said to Olena.

It surprised her that he could guess that and she automatically responded, "Olena."

"So gut, Olena. It haas been so long since we've haad a visitor," said Ogustus. Olena thought he meant it was good to have a visitor, but she had a difficult time understanding his accent.

"Eh, whatever," said Ovara.

Omarika still said nothing.

Olena already felt less frightened. Ogustus seemed as friendly as he first looked. Even the silent Omarika seemed less threatening now that she knew their names.

Only the girl, Ovara, bothered Olena. For some reason, Ovara appeared annoyed by Olena. She picked at Olena's dress and curls. Then she tried to fluff her own curls, but the sculpted metal did not move.

"Well, what do you want?" asked Ovara.

"She means," corrected Ogustus, "we are the Inhabitants and we are at your service. I surmise you have been given the ring for a specific purpose."

Olena remembered the Prismata telling her and Zandria that they would know the right time to use their gifts. She did not know if she was supposed to use the ring now, but the Inhabitants seemed ready to help her.

"I didn't know what would happen when I put the ring on." Olena decided to tell the truth. "I was cleaning my room, wishing I was somewhere else, and then I was here."

Ogustus said, "That's it then."

"Oh man," said Ovara. "We have to help her?"

Ogustus settled back onto his seat. "To the point, young one. You are going to help. Help her travel. Wherever here is, you should find a way to make it someplace else."

Forgetting her duties and the talk she recently finished with Kez, Olena became excited at the idea of travelling. "I want to go to the Southern Valley." She paused and scrunched her face in thought. "But how can you help me?"

"Watch," said Ovara.

She skipped over to the mirror and jumped without hesitation. Olena expected her to smash into it, but Ovara passed straight through.

Olena ran to the mirror. She could see Ovara talking to Kez and Sylvan.

"What's happening?" asked Olena.

"Doan worry, liddel lady. We cannot do anything you doan want us to do while we are in control. Our abilities can only improve your abilities. In a sense, it is still you out there, only in disguise."

Not sure how to feel about being stuck inside the ring, Olena, at least, liked the idea of being in disguise.

She said, "I guess that makes me the secret queen."

Chapter 8

"You know," said Olena, "I never did try this thing on.

Before Kez could respond, he watched Olena slip the bronze ring on her thumb. She disappeared instantly.

Kez tried to comprehend what happened. It looked like the ring sucked Olena inside it. His first thought was terrible, but then he remembered the ring was a gift from the Prismata, so he hoped it was good magic. Still, he had never seen anyone sucked through such a small hole. He watched Olena suddenly squish and stretch like a cloth would if pulled through such a hole.

Then, nothing. As soon as Olena disappeared, so did the ring.

Kez looked to Sylvan for any possible explanation. Before Sylvan could speak, another girl appeared in the exact spot Olena occupied a moment before.

She looked to be closer to Zandria's age, Kez guessed. She had thick black curly hair that came down close to her shoulders. She held it up with a scarf tied around her head and draped down her back. Her green eyes stood out on her dark-skinned face. From her brightly colored clothes, a baggy shirt and pants held with a wide sash, Kez wondered if she was a Southerner. Then he thought her style of dress looked too old, and much more traditional than the southerners he met since living at the castle. He also noticed she did not have the mysterious ring.

The stranger stood, looking at them.

"What have you done with Olena?" demanded Kez.

"Oh," said the girl. "You weren't supposed to see that."

He wanted to call for help, but Kez held his patience for an explanation.

Now Sylvan spoke, "We are advisors to the Queen of the Eastern Sky and responsible for her safety."

"Then relax. She's safe," said the girl. "For now, think of me as her substitute."

"Bad magic," said Kez. "I don't like this one bit. Who are you and where is Olena? This is your last chance."

"Okay. Take it easy. I'm Ovara. Your precious queen is with the other Inhabitants of the ring. She can come back whenever she wants, but she has to learn the rules first."

"What rules?" asked Sylvan.

Ovara did not respond to Sylvan. Kez already did not trust this girl.

He said, "I have a bad feeling about this."

"Normally, you wouldn't have any feeling," said Ovara. "Other people are not supposed to see when we trade places. I guess you two are in on the secret."

"What's she saying? I can't hear her," said Olena. She watched Ovara talking with Kez and Sylvan through the smoky green-tinted glass.

Ogustus stood next to her. "Listen with your heart," he said.

Olena did not understand what he meant, but she tried anyway. She closed her eyes and concentrated. After a moment, she knew exactly what was happening with Ovara. She did not hear the words exactly, but felt the emotion and suddenly had the memory of having the conversation.

"She wants Kez and Sylvan to keep this a secret."

Ogustus smiled, "Good. Then you have learned rule number one, listen with your heart."

"How many rules are there?" asked Olena. She wanted to learn them quickly. According to Ovara's conversation with Kez, that was the only way to get out of this strange bronze room.

"Eight hundred and seventy-seven," said Ogustus.

Omarika nodded in agreement.

"Ka!" said Olena. "I'll never learn all of them."

Ogustus said, "Doan worry child. Only the first four matter. The others will come with time and experience. You will be in control with the first four though."

That seemed much easier than learning hundreds of rules. Olena believed she could learn the first four without a problem. Unfortunately, with her desire to get away from everything else, she wound up right back in a lesson.

"Can you tell them to me?" asked Olena.

"Why doan I tell you a story instead," said Ogustus. "It will help you to know us better."

Olena did not want to hear a story, she wanted to be free.

That did not seem to affect Ogustus. He started telling the story, regardless of her feelings.

"Ovara was not always called Ovara. As you have surmised from our confusion, our names change depending on the wearer of the ring. They remain close to our originals, but changing the name is the first step in adapting to the new personality."

Olena thought about this for a moment. She did think it was strange that they had to ask each other's names. Somehow, they must have known her name started with an O. Because of that, their names apparently adapted to fit with hers.

Ogustus continued, "So, in her first life, Ovara had another name. She was born under the reign of the second Queen of the Southern Valley."

"Isis is the fifth," interrupted Olena.

Ogustus looked surprised. "Has it been that long? The last time we had a visitor was during the time of the Thrice Queen. Oh well, time passes."

"As the child of a farmer, she was destined to tend the fertile soil. Ovara did not want this. She did not like her life and dreamt of exploring the capital city. She wanted to see the marketplace and meet exotic peoples. She wanted to live in the Infinity Temple with the queen, not a low-ceilinged farmhouse made of dried mud and straw."

Olena thought Ovara's life sounded familiar. Instead of a farmer, her own father was a fisherman.

"Now an unhappy child sometimes tries to run away from her problems. That is what Ovara did. She left her poor, but loving, parents and wondered off to Hierakonpolis."

"Why would she leave her parents?" asked Olena. The idea of leaving her parents on purpose made Olena want to cry. She would give up anything, including being queen, to be with her parents again.

"Sometimes, we doan understand the value of what we have until we no longer have it," explained Ogustus.

He continued, "Hierakonpolis was a strange and wonderful place compared to the wet fields of home. In the beginning, Ovara was only amazed. By the end of the first day, she was still amazed, but also hungry. In her haste to get away, Ovara made no plans. She had nothing to eat and no place to sleep."

"While the citizens of Hierakonpolis are many and kind, it is easy to lose a child in the crowded streets. Ovara learned to survive on those streets with other orphans and castaways. She taught herself to survive. She became strong and independent."

"Yet, while she was strong, she also grew hard. True strength comes from your heart, but Ovara's heart was cold. She no longer felt love or had anyone to care for her. She only had herself. That is no kind of life."

What was the point of this story, wondered Olena. She already felt Ovara had a mean spirit. She did not think it was important to know any more about her. She wanted to know the other rules, but Ogustus did not seem to want to share.

He still had more of Ovara's story to tell.

"Now we doan know who created the ring. But, I believe it comes from the time of the Immortals, imbued with the Deep Magic. In any case, when it came to Ovara, the ring was already hundreds of years old and worn on many, many fingers."

"Nothing unusual happened the day Ovara found the ring. She was either begging or stealing food. She ducked into an alley to eat and saw something reflecting the bright afternoon sun."

"Of course, she was curious. Her first thought was how much food or protection she could trade it for. It did not occur to her to keep it for herself. It had been so long since she had any possessions and those things were long forgotten."

"Ovara slipped the ring on her finger for safe-keeping and found herself in a long hallway. Every part of it made of bronze exactly like the ring. The dark hall reflected shades of brown and green. Ovara lost her sense of fear surviving on the streets. I was not so brave my first time, but she immediately started down the hallway. She said she felt as if she walked for a day, but the hallway never ended."

"When I first put on the ring, Ovara was already here. Omarika joined us what seemed like not long after that. Even now, the liddel girl will not tell me who was here before her."

Ogustus shifted his immense weight on his stool.

"I assume there had to be other Inhabitants. There had to be someone before us. I calculate that Ovara was alone here for twenty or thirty years before me. She was already turned when I arrived."

"Turned?" asked Olena. "Into a statue?"

"I'm sorry if I did not make that clear," said Ogustus. "We were very much human before putting on the ring. At least two of us, as I cannot speak for Omarika and she woan speak for herself. She may be elven under that mask, for my guess."

Olena looked to Omarika. She did have a similar height and shape to Tym, or any of the other elves at Castle Empyrean, but Olena could not say for sure without seeing her face or ears. Omarika did nothing to reveal the truth.

"In a very short time, I noticed the change. I suspect because of your power as a queen, it has not affected you. Yet."

"I might become a statue?" This frightened Olena.

"That is the trick of the ring," said Ogustus. "It has the power to help you, but use it too much and you will be trapped."

"I'm already trapped. The other queens won't let me leave the castle and my powers don't work," said Olena.

"You may be surprised," said Ogustus. "For a short time, I served at the Chateau de la Belle Eternelle."

"Where is that?" asked Olena.

"I would say your lessons are failing you. You do not know the home of the Queen of the Western Sun?" asked Ogustus.

This disappointed Olena further. Cinderella or Snow White probably said the name of the castle during one of her lessons, but Olena forgot it.

She asked, "You know the western queen?"

"I knew a western queen. I sincerely doubt your queen is the same one from my time. The point being, I have been close to a queen and can recognize power. You have power. Knowing how to use it, maybe not so much."

Ogustus finished his story, "Now, you may understand Ovara's heart a liddel bedder. Do you remember the first rule? Listen with your heart. If you can do that in rhythm with Ovara's heart, you have mastered a little of the ring's power."

The big man leaned back on his chair and stopped moving. Olena noticed Omarika moved back to her pedestal as well. Then all was silent. Alone again, Olena turned back toward the mirror. She saw Ovara still with Kez and Sylvan in her bedroom. She thought she may have learned something from Ogustus.

She closed her eyes and tried to listen with her heart. At first, in the quiet bronze room, all she could hear was her own breathing. Then below that, she heard the steady thump of her own heart. Soon, another beat joined hers, a little harder and a little faster. This must be Ovara's heart, she guessed.

Olena did not open her eyes. She concentrated on Ovara's heartbeat. Then her bright bedroom replaced the darkness of her eyelids. Olena knew she did not open her eyes. She knew she did not leave the bronze room. She did not experience the same feeling of passing through the ring, no stomach-churning twisting.

Still, she stood in her bedroom in Castle Empyrean. She could clearly see Kez and Sylvan. Ovara looked very vibrant and alive as well. Almost the same as her statue form, but slightly different. She did not think they could see her though.

"Hey! Can you hear me?" asked Olena.

Kez and Sylvan did not respond, but Ovara looked around the room.

"Great. I didn't think she would figure it out that quick," said Ovara.

Olena discovered Ovara could hear her, but not see her.

"Who figured what out?" asked Kez. "Are you talking about Olena?"

Ovara did not respond. She looked preoccupied trying to find Olena. This made Olena want to try something else.

"Raise your right hand," said Olena.

"No," came the reply, but Olena did not see Ovara's mouth move this time. She realized she was not moving her own mouth. They must be communicating with their hearts, she thought.

"I said raise your right hand," repeated Olena.

No reply this time. Instead, Ovara reluctantly raised her right hand. She did not look happy to obey and quickly let her arm flop back down.

"Happy?" asked Ovara.

Sylvan interrupted their thought-speak, "Are you communicating with our queen?"

A cold breeze covered Olena. She guessed this is what Ovara's heart felt like all the time. It made her sad that Ovara had no one. At least Olena still had Zandria and Kez, plus she kept getting new friends like Sylvan and William.

"Sure," Ovara answered Sylvan's question. "That's the power of the ring. She says I'm in charge and you're not supposed to tell anyone what's happened."

"I never said that," shouted Olena.

"They don't know that," Ovara thought back to her.

Kez looked surprised to Olena, but he seemed to be accepting Ovara's explanation. Now Ovara looked around the room, maybe trying to decide if she wanted to change clothes. Apparently, she did not find what she was looking for and came back to the center of the room.

To Kez and Sylvan, she said, "Let's take a little trip."

As Ovara raised both of her arms, palms outward, Olena realized what she was trying to do.

"No," demanded Olena. "You can't do that. It doesn't work."

Then Ovara touched her thumbs together. She turned her hands inward and almost before her fingers touched, a triangle of light appeared in front of her. The Walking Portal grew large enough for Ovara. She grabbed Sylvan and stepped through. Olena saw Kez hesitate, but then jump through a second before the portal closed. Olena felt herself pulled along too.

The Walking Portal actually worked. Olena could not believe it. She could not get it to go at all, not even a flash of light, and Ovara did it on her first try. It had to be the power of the ring, she suspected. Still, it did not make her like Ovara anymore because of it.

Olena did not recognize where they were. Behind her she saw the tall grass of the central plains, but nothing else for miles, not even Castle Empyrean. In front of her, she saw an enormous dirt mound. The hill rose up sharply and stretched off to the left and right. Olena thought it might be a gate or boundary of some type. It looked well cared for and had no tracks or footprints on any of the dirt that she could see, except for one spot.

In the middle of the ridge, Olena could make out the tiniest trickle of water. The rivulet spilled down the hillside and disappeared in the high plains grass. Could this be the Brygos River that Isis talked about, Olena wondered.

Then Ovara said aloud, "Home at last," but she did not sound particularly happy about it.

Ovara trudged up the hillside, dislodging dirt and leaving deep indentions in the smooth surface. She held Sylvan by one arm, like a doll. Kez made it up the loose slope much easier with his smaller size.

From here, Olena could see the beginnings of the Southern Valley.

On the south side of the hill, the Brygos spread out across a delta to form an enormous lake. Farms and crops surrounded the lake as far as Olena could see. Where the lake turned back into a stream, she saw a tall, narrow tower. She knew from Ovara's heart that this was called an obelisk and they were everywhere in the Southern Valley. Far off on the horizon, Olena could see giant triangle shaped buildings which Ovara called the pyramids. Olena guessed they had to be massive if she could see them from this far.

"I told you not to do that," scolded Olena. "I'm supposed to be in control."

Ovara thought back, "You're the one that wanted to travel."

Chapter 9

Reading a person's heart seemed confusing to Olena. Ovara's thoughts and memories mingled with her own. She had a difficult time keeping them separate. Olena now had things from Ovara's head that made it feel like it was her own knowledge. She did not understand how she could know the lake at the bottom of the mound was called Nata Playa. Also, she knew it was half the size that Ovara remembered it to be.

This bothered Olena for two reasons. One, she could not imagine this giant body of water to be any bigger. She guessed with its size now that it would take an entire day to walk from here to the opposite side going around the edge. The other thing that bothered her is whether the process worked both ways. Did Ovara have all of her thoughts and memories, Olena wondered? Did she have the ability to block things from the strange girl?

Olena opened her eyes. She felt maybe this was one of the tricks of the ring. She wondered if she concentrated too much, would she remain trapped in the ring. She looked at her surroundings. The dark metal room felt cold and empty. Besides the now still statues of Ogustus and Omarika and the mirror, she saw nothing else. Olena preferred the sights and sounds of the outside world, even if she could only experience them through Ovara's senses.

She started to concentrate again and passed back into the light. In a way, Olena felt like she was riding on Ovara's back. She knew Ovara was not big enough to carry her. Still, she went everywhere Ovara went and seemed to look at things over her shoulder.

"Strange, huh?" thought Ovara. That answered Olena's question as to whether Ovara could read her thoughts. At least for now, the connection seemed to go both ways.

Olena said, "Sorry. I meant strange because I don't know you."

"I think you will get to know me pretty well some day," thought Ovara.

In the short time Olena had broken the connection, Ovara climbed down the slope. She now walked on the rich black soil at the edge of the lake. Kez splashed in the water to get a drink.

"I wouldn't get too close," said Ovara.

Kez turned his back to the lake to ask, "Why?"

Behind him, Olena watched a gigantic mouth full of hundreds of pointed teeth slowly rise out of the water. She thought the huge mouth made Kez look quite small. It had room for him, Ovara and herself to swallow in one bite.

"That's why," said Ovara, pointing at the enormous golden crocodile that the mouth belonged to. It completely surfaced from the lake.

The quzzak turned around in time to see the massive jaws snap closed. Kez missed being eaten by only an instant. His reflexes allowed him to back flip out of the way at the last second. He scurried behind Ovara, and then climbed up on her shoulder for safety.

This did not seem to be much safer, thought Olena. The crocodile, as long as six Friesians end-to-end, started to lumber toward Ovara. He slowly opened his mouth, determined to have breakfast.

"That's enough," said a new female voice.

The crocodile did not stop. Ovara looked around for the other voice, but Olena spotted her first. At least she thought she did. A large round head poked out of the water behind the crocodile.

The female creature spoke again. Olena saw two huge, flat teeth in her curved mouth. She said, "Sobek, call him off."

Apparently, this water animal now spoke to the tiny crocodile that Olena had previously not noticed resting on the female's wide back.

The little white crocodile said, "As you wish." Then to the golden crocodile, "Tawakafa."

Whatever the word meant, the golden crocodile stopped immediately. The frighteningly long creature turned around and sank back into the lake. Then the new animal with the tiny crocodile on its back came up on the shore. Ovara's memory told Olena that her people called this creature a hippopotamus. To match her round head, the hippopotamus had an equally round body and stood twice as tall as Ovara.

Olena could tell that Ovara felt hippopotami were dangerous, but this one seemed friendly.

"I am Taweret," said the gentle beast. "My companion is the Mighty Sobek."

The idea of the tiny white crocodile being called mighty tickled Olena. She thought he looked small enough to be a baby. Still, he had power over the giant crocodiles, apparently.

'I would say I'm honored to meet you, but you almost let us get eaten," said Ovara.

Olena could not believe how disrespectful Ovara was being. She understood Taweret and Sobek were among the most revered animals in the Southern Valley. Ovara's heart told Olena that the hippopotamus protected mothers and children, while Sobek ruled over the golden crocodiles. He probably chose William's friend Aleta when she came to fight in the Rockhorn Battle, Olena guessed. Ovara's thoughts quickly confirmed that Sobek matches all of his crocodiles with their riders and it is quite a ceremony.

"You are an insolent child," said Taweret. "Yet you carry greatness within you. I sense the power of a queen."

Sobek added, "There is something about her." Then he said to Ovara, "Whatever secret you are hiding, there are people in our land that may want to harm you to discover the truth. Be wise in your journey."

Olena could see that Ovara believed she could protect herself without their warnings.

"Tell them thank you," thought Olena.

"Thank you," said Ovara. Then she thought back at Olena, "Stop telling me what to do."

Taweret nodded her large head in acknowledgement of Ovara's thanks. She said, "Because you have shown gratitude, I have a gift for you. Follow the scarlet ibis to your destination."

Then Taweret waddled back into the water. Sobek disappeared last as they swam deeper into Nata Playa.

"Some gift," said Ovara. "I don't see any birds, let alone an ibis, which are always white by the way."

"It sounded helpful to me," said Kez. "Maybe Olena is at our destination."

Olena screamed, "I'm right here."

"I'm Olena," escaped Ovara's mouth. Olena thought maybe with enough emotion, she could talk through Ovara. Maybe she could take control? Ovara quickly slapped her hands over her mouth to keep Olena from saying anything else. This made her drop Sylvan to the ground.

Kez leapt down to assist his wooden friend. Olena could not get Ovara to do anything else.

"That's it," demanded Kez. "We are not going anywhere until you explain. I don't care if another crocodile comes and eats us. Who are you and where is Olena?"

Olena could feel Ovara relent, but only a little. She explained that the ring had the power to change her appearance in order to travel in disguise.

"But it must be broken, because Olena can't change back," finished Ovara.

"That's a lie," thought Olena. "You're keeping me here, like a prisoner."

Ovara let Olena understand that she only wanted to see her home again. She had nothing to do with Olena not being able to turn back into herself. Then Olena remembered that she needed to learn the rules in order to master the ring. She did not think Ovara was lying to her, but she still did not trust her completely.

Sylvan and Kez seemed to accept the explanation, however. They started walking with Ovara toward one of the villages they had seen from the hilltop. How could they trust her so easily, thought Olena. Maybe they were too worried about her and it clouded their judgment?

"Perhaps, at our destination, we will find someone to fix the ring," said Sylvan.

A loud squawking interrupted the beginning of this conversation. Then a red feathered bird fluttered out of the nearby marsh grass. Olena thought if looked like a seagull, except with longer legs and a longer neck. The bird also had a long curved beak. She guessed this to be the scarlet ibis because of its beautiful color.

"That's the bird Taweret told us to follow," thought Olena. "But is her gift the bird itself or the destination that it will lead us to?"

Then the ibis flew out over the lake. It continued in the opposite direction from where they were going.

"Too bad," said Ovara. "I guess we're not going to find out. I'm hungry and the closest village is this way."

Ovara kept going and did not look back. Olena wondered if the girl cared about anything except herself.

Away from the swampy edges of the lake, they started walking through tall rows of green wheat. Ovara's knowledge of farming surprised Olena and told her that this wheat still had a long time to grow before harvest. Olena could not imagine the crops growing anymore because they were already taller than her head.

Wheat seemed to be the main crop of the southern farmers. It came in several varieties and colors. Olena learned that most crops made for food, but a few special farmers grew a silky type used in clothes, sold mostly in Hierakonpolis, the capital city.

Hierakonpolis is where Ovara wanted to go. Olena could tell she did not want to visit farms or even see her real family. She considered the city to be her home. Ovara did not seem to even like walking through the fields. Olena started to think maybe Ovara had some unfinished business in the city.

What could be waiting for Ovara, Olena wondered. From her lessons, Olena guessed it had been at least a thousand years since Ovara lived in Hierakonpolis. Maybe she did not realize how much time had passed while she was trapped in the Bronze Ring. Whatever her reasons, Ovara managed to keep them hidden from Olena. She tried to read her mind, but felt blocked. Apparently, the connection is not like an open book. Olena figured her weak magic abilities allowed Ovara to block some things from her.

Near the end of the day, they finally approached the village. Soon the farmers, who had been tending their fields, joined them on the last stretch of the walk into the village.

Everyone seemed friendly. The village children immediately wanted to play with Kez and Sylvan. One father even invited Ovara to have dinner with his family. Olena sensed her desire for food outweighed her desire for solitude. Ovara reluctantly accepted the invitation.

They ate a simple meal of bread and kafee. The farmers made both the food and drink from the very wheat they tended each day in the field. They ground the mature grains into dust that went into the bread. She discovered they baked the bread in small ovens made of dried mud bricks. For the kafee, they first cooked the grain, then grinded it to mix with the sparkling water of the Nata Playa.

At dinner, they drank their kafee cold, but in the morning, most farmers preferred it hot to help them shake off their sleep. Olena enjoyed trying new foods. Not until breakfast the next day did it occur to her that she did not taste the food with her own mouth. Everything seemed so hot and delicious, but only in her memory. Most of all, she did not feel hungry. Olena could not believe the unusual power of the ring.

When they finished eating, the kind farmer insisted on helping them prepare for their continued travels. He pulled a greasy black stick from his hip pouch.

"You will need this when you enter the desert," he said.

Ovara knew what it was and held her face up to the man. He drew a line under each eye, similar to those on his own tanned face. Olena thought it was funny to see men wearing make-up, but she understood it was to fight the glare of the intensely bright southern sun.

"Come here monkey," the farmer said to Kez. He reached for Kez, but the quzzak jumped clear.

Kez said, "I'll have you know I am no monkey. They are untrustworthy and dirty."

The farmer did not seem to care about the difference. He said, "Either way, you need this to keep from going blind."

When the farmer finished, Kez had two thick lines, one under each eye that ended in downward curls. Ovara and Olena laughed together at this sight.

"Now you will be the king of monkeys," laughed the farmer.

"Still not a monkey," said Kez. He looked annoyed, staring at his reflection near the water's edge. This village had been built on the shore of Nata Playa.

The farmer gave Ovara a small pouch for food. Then Olena reminded her about Sylvan. Ovara found him surrounded by several young children. They laughed and cheered when he walked on his own. This made Olena want to play with them.

"Is it a toy?" asked the farmer.

Sylvan answered for himself, "I am advisor to the Queen of the Eastern Sky since the Third House of Soria Moria."

The look on the farmer's face told Olena that he did not believe Sylvan. Olena suggested that Ovara hide Sylvan in her pouch for now. She thought this was better to not raise any suspicions.

Back at the shore, the farmer went to work on an amazing looking wheel. Pieces of metal had been bent and set in place on the large wheel. The flat row of metal spiraled in on itself, ending in a hole at the center of the wheel.

The farmer lowered the wheel into the lake only far enough to get the edge wet. Then he turned a crank that started the wheel spinning. Olena watched the outer row of metal scoop up water. As it turned, the water sloshed along the spiral path toward the center of the wheel. After a moment of watching the hypnotic pattern, Olena wanted to see the other side. Ovara moved behind the wheel. The water spilled through the center hole and ran along a trough to the village well.

The creativity of the southern people impressed Olena, yet she felt concern from Ovara.

"You have to fill your well from the lake?" she asked.

"I do only what my father did, as did his father before him," answered the farmer.

"I don't understand," said Ovara. "The Brygos was always flowing. We never had want of water. Our well always stayed full."

"Those days are long past. It has been at least three hundred years since the River of Life delivered on its promise," explained the farmer. "We are lucky now to have enough to keep our crops alive. Beyond the Unending Desert, strangers have blocked our river. For too long, our queen tolerated them, but now those monsters want our land as well."

Olena could feel anger swelling up in Ovara's heart. Ovara acted like she did not need anyone, but news of the river affected her deeply. Olena searched Ovara's memories to find a reason. The southerners called the Brygos the River of Life because it actually provided life. Maybe Ovara pretended not to care. Still, she knew the river was too important to let anyone keep it from her people.

"It's time to go," said Ovara.

"Now where?" asked Kez.

"To the Infinity Temple," she replied.

After saying goodbye and thanking the farmer for his scarce food, Ovara led them south.

Olena thought, "Are you going to talk to Queen Isis?"

"I have to say something," Ovara thought back. "I will not believe any Queen of the Southern Valley would allow this to happen."

As they continued closer to the obelisk at the southern tip of Nata Playa, the crops grew smaller and less frequent. Swamps replaced the fertile black soil. Olena did not like the feel of the mud seeping into Ovara's shoes. This seemed to make Ovara purposely step into deeper puddles.

When they reached the smooth white obelisk, Olena saw something surprising resting on its pointed tip. High above their heads sat the scarlet ibis. The bird looked down at them for a moment. Then it flew off toward the south over the waiting desert. She could not believe this was the same bird, but it had to be. They saw no other birds anywhere near Nata Playa.

Beyond the obelisk, Olena could see only sand.

"Is this the Unending Desert?" she asked Ovara.

Ovara said, "Everything from here to the temple used to be farmland. The Unending Desert is south of Hierakonpolis."

Before they started following the Brygos toward Hierakonpolis, Olena took one last look at the obelisk. It stood much taller than the palm trees of Banookanook. It looked like one solid piece of stone. Who carved it, wondered Olena.

She thought she could feel some kind of energy radiating from it, but Ovara did not wait for her to study it more.

Ovara and Kez walked along the struggling Brygos. It looked much more like a brook than a river. Olena thought she could easily straddle it with a foot on each side.

Soon, they could no longer see the farms behind them or anything ahead. This reminded Olena of the Wastelands in the east. However, she gladly would have traded this scorching sun for those strong winds. At least then, they had the option of walking in the narrow crevices to stay out of the wind.

Kez kept squinting into the distance. Referring to his eyeliner, he said, "This stuff really works. I can see a city."

Chapter 10

The city Kez saw turned out to be only a mirage. The bright sun reflected off the hot sand and made it seem like Hierakonpolis was much closer. Where the city appeared to be, they now stood in the middle of a scorching desert.

Olena could not feel the heat directly, but she could feel its effects on Ovara's body. Mostly, she felt tired and angry. Surprisingly, Ovara shared the last of their water with Kez. Olena did not expect sharing like this from her.

Especially now with the water gone, Olena knew they had to find shade somehow. She urged Ovara to keep walking. Then Olena wondered why they could not drink from the thin ribbon of water that used to be the Brygos.

"It's not fair," said Ovara. "The Brygos used to be so deep and too wide for me to swim across. It's probably not even safe to drink now with all this sand."

"Things have changed," said Kez.

"You don't have to tell me," Ovara replied.

Now Olena could feel Ovara wanted to quit. She did not like what happened to her homeland and did not know what to do about it. It scared Olena that Ovara might simply sit down in the desert and surrender.

"We can't stop now," demanded Olena.

"What difference does it make?" thought Ovara.

"I don't know," responded Olena, "but let's get to Isis. She is already working to fix the problem. Something like this happened to my home. One man, who turned into a baby, saved all of it. Maybe there is something the four of us can do."

Ovara dropped down to sit on the hot sand. She said, "We're too late."

She did not appear to want to move. Kez looked concerned. Then Ovara tossed Sylvan on the ground in front of her. He struggled to stand up, slipping in the sand. Once he made it to his feet, the sand continued to move around him.

Olena looked closer. It seemed as if the sand started to bubble. Something underneath must be trying to force its way out, guessed Olena. This made her both nervous and curious at the same time.

Sylvan's little head spun in circles as he examined the moving sand all around his little body.

He said, "We should be going now."

"I think you're right," agreed Ovara.

She quickly jumped up and brushed the sand off her pants and then rubbed her hands together to clear them. When she reached for Sylvan, a small creature with a pointed tail popped out of the ground. It tried to sting Ovara's hand with its tail as she pulled Sylvan to safety.

"Scorpions," screamed Ovara.

Then hundreds of the frightening creatures burst up from the ground like a bubbling fountain. The hundreds of scorpions rapidly multiplied into thousands. Olena realized they must have disturbed their nest, usually hidden safely from the blistering sun. The hungry creatures now swarmed after their potential meal. She watched the golden sand quickly turn black from the rush of the little monsters. There were so many, she could not see the ground beneath them.

"Run, run, run," Olena kept shouting.

"What does it look like I'm doing?" Ovara yelled back.

Kez could barely keep Ovara's pace. Countless sharp claws nipped at his tail. Still, the quzzak and his human companion ran as fast as they could. The flood of scorpions kept coming after them as they climbed a sandy ridge.

Then as suddenly as the scorpions appeared, they began burrowing back into the sand. Many of them did not move quickly enough and fell victim to the huge flock of ibis that swooped down from the sky. The scorpions must have sensed the aerial attack and tried to retreat.

The same scarlet ibis that Olena saw twice before now led hundreds of white ibis to their rescue. The birds nabbed up the bite-size scorpions in their curved beaks. The roar of so many flapping bird wings drowned out all other sound.

As the last of the scorpions burrowed or were swallowed, the ibis flock separated. The birds flew in different directions like the clouds parting after a storm. Soon the ground and sky both looked clear. From the top of the dune, Olena tried to follow the flight path of the mysterious red bird. She watched it sail over an enormous city. This time, the city did not disappear like a mirage.

"We made it," said Ovara. When she wanted to give up, she must not have realized how close they were.

Across the horizon, Olena could see one, two and three story buildings. In between these, she spotted many statues, obelisks and triangle pyramids. The closer they got, the bigger Hierakonpolis seemed. Their view had been blocked by the last sand dune. Ovara almost gave up when they were so close.

The stream known as the Brygos River sloped downhill toward a wide tunnel. Olena could not believe the tunnel opening looked wider than the length of Banookanook.

"That's Abydos," thought Ovara.

Olena stared into its total darkness. The trickle of Brygos seeped meekly out of its mouth and flowed up the hill toward them.

Ovara continued, "The Brygos used to fill the entire tunnel. The rush of water could be felt vibrating your feet as it passed under the whole city."

Losing that much water could easily destroy a land, thought Olena. She lived by water for the first six years of her life and she loved it. She knew how important water could be. It made her sad to see such an amazing place deprived of it.

Abydos seemed to call to her, not with a voice, but with emotion. Olena wanted to know what might be in the complete blackness.

"The dead," said Ovara aloud.

"What's that?" asked Kez.

"Abydos, under the city, is the home of the dead. Some say the tunnels under the Infinity Temple lead down there," explained Ovara.

This made Olena quickly change her mind. She did not want to go to the home of the dead. Still, Abydos pulled at her. Thankfully, Ovara turned them toward the city.

They walked along the wide streets. Every cut-stone house seemed to have large clay jars by each door, filled with a variety of foods or possessions. The Hierakonpolitans covered their walls with beautiful paintings. Different walls appeared to tell different stories. Maybe past adventures or battles, guessed Olena. Other walls simply had bright solid colors of red, yellow or blue.

Only the pyramids and obelisks had no paintings on the outside. Ovara's memory told Olena that the pyramids had paintings inside, but they were very old. She thought they were so old that no one knew who painted them or even built the pyramids. Because they were sacred places, the queen forbid anyone to go inside them.

Now they passed close to another white obelisk. Olena could feel the same radiating energy again. Ovara could not explain this and said she could not feel anything.

This reminded Olena of the scarlet ibis, who seemed to like perching atop the tall stone. She searched the sky, but saw no sign of the bird. More and more, Olena believed they needed to follow the ibis wherever it might be going. Ovara did not share this opinion. Now Olena worried that they might not ever see it again.

Ovara led them toward what she called the marketplace. Olena could only think of the Edge Town Market with six, sometimes ten, carts where her father used to sell his fish. Ovara's heart did not prepare her for the Hierakonpolis Market.

As they drew closer, they started seeing more and more people. It amazed Olena how some dressed in magnificent robes while others barely wore anything at all. She noticed their dark skinned bodies covered with scented oils, probably to protect their skin from the sun. Most of the men and women kept their black hair cut short.

Still, the Hierakonpolitans that impressed Olena the most looked the least human. These southerners had human bodies, but animal heads. However, the other people treated them no different than normal humans.

Olena recognized the head of a hippopotamus. This woman walked, surrounded by four men that looked like guards. Maybe she is someone important, wondered Olena.

Others that walked toward the market included cat-headed men and women. Olena loved their swishing tails. These cats stepped out of the way when a strong looking man with a lion's head came down the street.

The snake heads frightened Olena with their narrow eyes. Crocodile headed people did not make her feel much better. In the crowd, she also saw some cow heads with long horns and hawk-headed men. Ovara had to tell her that the skinny black dog heads were called jackals. She assured Olena, at least in her time, the jackals were more dangerous than the snakes.

No one else seemed worried or acted unusual with these animal-people. Olena remembered Queen Isis had a few hand maidens with cat heads, but they had not visited

Castle Empyrean in a long time. She loved that about Empyrean. So many amazing things existed outside of Banookanook. Sometimes, she wanted to go home, but other times, she never wanted to go back there. She felt like she could travel across Empyrean for years and still never meet all of its inhabitants.

Before they entered the market, Olena noticed an unusual statue on the street corner.

"There's one of these on each of the four corners of the market," said Ovara. She seemed excited by them, but Olena could not glean anything more from the girl's memory.

Olena studied the statue more closely. The disgusting figure did not look like it belonged in this beautiful city. Almost shapeless, the figure had been carved with folds of fat over its round belly. Olena thought maybe it could have been a tall creature that had its bones removed. With no bones, all the skin collapsed into a pile and the stone carver made the statue from that.

The face looked no better. Whatever the creature might be, it was never human. Olena could not tell if it was supposed to have two or three eyes. The mouth definitely had sharp teeth, though. Also, she saw strange markings on its forehead that looked like writing, but none that the queens had ever taught to Olena.

"I believe I recognize those symbols," said Sylvan. "Please hold me close, miss."

Ovara lifted Sylvan up to see the face of the statue.

After a moment, Sylvan said, "I had hoped the stories were not true. In the time before the First Queen, when the Forgotten Evil ruled Empyrean, he had four lieutenants. They led his armies and did most of his evil work."

"What happened to them?" Ovara asked for Olena. Olena feared she could guess the answer right in front of them.

Sylvan continued, "When the First Queen defeated their master, the four slaves were cast into deep pits and sealed away. Only a seal of great power could contain them. A seal like this."

Olena realized these lieutenants were trapped in deep holes, one at each corner of the market. She guessed the market did not exist when the statues were put in place. Most people probably did not even know what the statues meant. Olena hoped that no one could ever open these seals.

Not wanting to dwell on this, Ovara took them into the market.

Olena expected the Edge Town Market, so this place left her in awe. Rows and rows of booths and tables filled the huge space surrounded by the four statues. High walls with many archways marked the boundaries of the marketplace. Olena could not see all the way from one side to the other. Hierakonpolitans crowded every aisle, buying and trading the goods offered there.

Above them, Olena saw long cotton sheets draped across cedar beams. This provided shade for the market and trapped an unexpected cool breeze beneath it. She took a moment to scan for the scarlet ibis, but did not see it. However, she did see four tiny hawks. They looked like Guardian Hawks from Castle Empyrean. Sadly, they perched on one of the beams overhead and Olena could not get close enough to talk to them.

They wandered the aisles tasting foods and looking at jewelry and clothes. Olena could feel the tension ease in Ovara's heart. Whatever she had been searching for, she must have found it here. Maybe Ovara needed to be someplace familiar to feel safe, thought Olena.

When they turned into the next row, the wrecked display shocked Olena. Someone's entire booth had been destroyed. Broken sticks lay everywhere, but most of them still hung together in what must have been a very intricate structure. At the top, rested the scarlet ibis. It took wing as soon as Olena saw it.

"We have to follow that bird," said Olena.

"Why?" retorted Ovara.

"I don't know, but we have to," demanded Olena.

Ovara thought, "Because a talking hippo told us to? What if a crocodile told us we'd be safe hiding in his mouth? Would you get in?"

"That's different," Olena said. "Sometimes, you have to do things because you believe in them."

"Well, I believe I am going to stay right here," finished Ovara.

While they had this internal discussion, the four miniature hawks started to circle overhead. Olena recognized Captain Aeran, who she first met the day of the Rockhorn Battle.

"Aeran," Olena forced the name out of Ovara's mouth. The hawks sailed down and landed on the wooden wreckage.

"Forgive me," said Aeran, "but do I know you?"

Kez spoke up first, "I am Advisor to the Queen of the Eastern Sky." Referring to Sylvan, "My associate and I are escorting this young lady at the request of Queen Olena."

The hawk cocked his head to the side. He said, "Strange. For a moment, from up there, I thought she was the young queen."

Ovara did not want to explain further. Olena thought it might be too complicated and agreed.

Apparently, Kez agreed as well. He changed the subject by asking, "What are the four of you doing so far from home?"

Before Aeran could answer, a tall figure with the head of a hawk interrupted them.

"Forgive me, but I have some important information for the young lady and you, as well, Captain," he said. Olena felt something unusual from this man. He seemed different from the other hawkmen they had seen, but she could not determine why. He was definitely taller than the others, she could tell.

"And who are you?" asked Aeran.

"Call me Horus and call me friend," said the bird-man.

Aeran and the other hawks bowed respectfully when they heard the name. Apparently, Ovara recognized his name as well. Olena could feel her becoming annoyed. From Ovara's memories, she guessed Horus to be another ancient protector like Taweret or Sobek.

The bird-man spoke to Ovara, "My spies have learned the name of the peoples from the far south. The Arcosaurans are not all against Empyrean, only those that serve Emperor Li-Am. If you should happen to speak with the Queen of the Southern Valley, this is something you should tell her."

Horus finished with a wink, or maybe it was only a normal bird blink. Olena wondered if he knew she was really a queen. Like Taweret, he probably did, but did not risk giving away her identity. In any event, he guessed correctly that they intended to speak with Queen Isis.

He continued talking to the small hawks, "My brothers, I know you suffered a great loss this morning, but there is still time. The object you seek is being carried to the far south as well. Those soldiers intend to deliver it to their Emperor in Arcenland and they only have a few hours lead on you. I suspect they do not yet realize its full significance."

The Guardian Hawks did not hesitate. They immediately flew south without another word.

Whatever object they were after, Olena guessed it must be very important to them.

"They seemed to trust you," said Ovara.

The noble looking bird man leaned in close. He said, "We birds have a sense for these things. If you believe you can trust us, then you should. Maybe someone else told you something like this?"

How could he know that Taweret told them to follow a bird, wondered Olena. She assumed this is what he meant about trusting birds.

Then Horus slipped into the crowd and disappeared as quickly as he appeared.

Olena tried looking for him. Then she spotted the scarlet ibis again, several aisles away from them.

"Can we follow him now?" asked Olena.

Ovara relented. She said, "Fine, but don't blame me if it leads you straight to Abydos."

Chapter 11

Olena knew the red bird wanted to be followed. Still, it did not slow down as Ovara and Kez pushed their way through the crowded market. Ovara slammed into a lion-headed man.

"Watch where you're going, child," he growled.

"Sorry," she said without looking back.

Finally, they made it out onto the smooth sand street. The ibis circled once, and then headed down one of the long avenues. The bird stayed far enough ahead that Ovara had to constantly run not to lose sight of it.

Ovara wanted to give up the chase. Olena urged her to continue. She thought, "Have faith."

"That's it," boomed Ogustus' voice inside her head and in the bronze room.

Olena opened her eyes and broke her connection with Ovara. After the bright southern sun, Olena could barely see in the lonely darkness. She waited a moment for her eyes to adjust.

"Did you say something?" Olena asked the unmoving statue of Ogustus.

He did not respond. Still, Olena believed he said "That's it" when she told Ovara to have faith. She wondered if this had something to do with the ring's rules.

Since Ogustus did not answer, Olena concentrated on Ovara again. When she made her connection, the bright day almost blinded her. It did not help that the ibis swooped down a side alley. The narrow twists and turns made Olena feel sick and disoriented.

Thankfully, Ovara stopped and Olena could get her bearings. Then Olena realized why they had stopped.

In front of them, three children, all younger than Olena, scrounged through garbage. They looked to be searching for food. They wore torn clothes and smelled like they had not bathed in weeks.

Olena felt bad for the kids, but she could feel Ovara's heart breaking. Then anger replaced the despair. Ovara reached into her pouch and gave the kids the last of their own food. Olena understood Ovara would rather let herself starve than see that happen to another child. This made Olena think that maybe Ovara faked her tough attitude to keep from getting hurt.

Now, Olena took a chance to see where they were. When she broke the connection, she lost track of their progress. Trying to figure it out, Olena knew she could not find her way back to the marketplace from here on her own. Ahead, she could see the scarlet ibis perched on a window ledge, waiting. Then behind her, she thought she glimpsed two figures following them. They looked like jackals.

She waited, but nothing happened. Olena thought she must have imagined the two jackal-headed men watching them. No one came down the alley. Again, she guessed, her anxiety over her magic caused her to see people that were not really there like those eyes in the bushes back at the Palace by the Sea. She decided not to volunteer this to Ovara.

Ovara finished with the kids. "Now where, bird?" she asked the ibis.

The ibis continued through the maze of side streets. It moved slower at each turn, apparently trying to decide which way to go. At the end of a particularly skinny alley, the scarlet ibis disappeared behind a canvas curtain that served as the door to a well-hidden house.

Ovara rushed in after the bird without knocking or asking if anyone was home. Olena could not see the bird anywhere in the cluttered room. Amidst an assortment of vibrantly colored pillows and cushions, she saw a variety of gadgets. Some looked broken, some unfinished, some completely unusual. They were made of everything from wood and metal to a polished cow skull.

Nowhere could Olena find the scarlet ibis, except for a crude painting on one wall. It had red wings and a long curved beak, but one leg was longer than the other. Olena thought maybe a young child drew this because the drawing was not very good. Then she noticed a single red feather drifting down in front of the wall. She wondered if the real bird turned into this drawing.

Ogustus' voice interrupted her thoughts, "Or maybe this drawing turned into the bird?"

Olena's mind snapped to the bronze room. Ogustus sat waiting for her with a broad smile across his face. This time, he did not hide in his statue form.

"I think you have discovered it, liddel lady," he said.

"What did I discover?" asked Olena. "The next rule?"

He leaned forward as if he wanted to tell her a secret. "What made you follow the bird?"

"I don't know," shrugged Olena. "It seemed like the right thing to do."

"And now, what has happened to birdie?"

She looked around the room, hoping Ogustus would give her a hint. He did not and Omarika did not help either.

"I think," Olena clicked her teeth with her tongue, "I believe it turned into the painting."

"Back where it came from, eh?" Ogustus lumbered down from his seat. He moved very close, so much that Olena felt like she needed to step back. "You have faith then?"

She thought about this for a moment. To her, that word had a deeper meaning and she did not think she fully understood it. Her father used to talk about faith, especially at times when the fish were scarce or the storms were bad. He said to have faith and everything would be alright. Olena believed him and she believed in other things she could not prove. That seemed good enough for her.

"Yes," she answered. "I have faith."

"Then you have learned the second rule," said Ogustus.

He bumped her with his protruding stomach. Olena thought she would crash into the mirror. Instead, she splashed through it like falling on her back in the ocean.

For a moment, Olena could not breathe. Then she stood in the middle of the cluttered room with the ibis painting on the wall. The Bronze Ring slipped off her thumb and clinked on the stone floor.

"You're back," exclaimed Kez.

Olena could not feel her connection with Ovara. She could feel the hot air and a slight hunger pang.

"I'm back," cheered Olena. Kez jumped up into her arms for a big hug. Then she quickly scooped up the ring and carefully dropped it into her pocket. She did not want anybody else to get tricked into it.

"Oh, hello," said a boy's voice.

Olena turned around to see a tall skinny boy standing in the doorway. His pale skin looked odd compared to all of the dark skinned people Olena had seen in this land. She guessed he must be about sixteen years old. His glasses made him look older and smarter, but his messy hair made him look younger.

"Weren't you a different person a moment ago?" he asked.

Kez spoke up, "Trust me. They are very different."

"In either case, I'm still me. Karl Lumpkin," said the boy.

He stuck out a hand in greeting. Olena took it and curtsied as Cinderella taught her.

"Pleased to meet you. I'm Olena."

"And what are you doing here? Wait, let me guess, you're travelling in disguise?" Karl seemed to be trying hard to guess. "No, that's not it."

Olena giggled and then finished her introductions, "These are my friends Sylvan and Kez."

Karl approached Kez. He tripped over his own feet and crashed into a table. He acted like nothing happened, saying, "Fantastic, a quzzak."

"You know my kind?" asked Kez, looking somewhat pleased.

"Not yet," said Karl.

What a strange response, thought Olena. Karl seemed very unusual.

"What does that mean?" she asked.

The older boy looked down at her from his foot and a half taller height. He said, "I expect you will know what it means before I do, even if it takes a hundred years."

"You are strange," laughed Olena.

"Quite," agreed Kez.

"It's okay," said Karl, adjusting his glasses. "I get that a lot because I've done all this before. The only thing I can tell you is it doesn't end well for me."

Olena's imagination raced. She believed the ibis led her to this house. If Karl Lumpkin lives here, then she was supposed to meet him. This must be Taweret's gift. The boy seemed to be talking gibberish, but Olena wondered if maybe he could predict the future. He acted like he knew about things that had not happened yet. Olena could not think of a way to test if he was telling the truth.

Then Karl said, "Now, Your Majesty, do you have the ring?"

In surprise, Olena almost said "Yes". She started to think she did not need to test him.

Even if he recognized her as a Queen, she could not guess how he knew about the Bronze Ring.

"You can trust me," Karl reassured her. "I told myself you'd be coming."

Another weird saying, thought Olena. Karl Lumpkin both amused her and made her nervous. Something about him also made her trust him. Olena decided, on faith, to tell him everything.

She started with Banookanook and wanted to tell how she became queen. Karl already knew that, so she skipped to more recent events and showed him the ring.

"May I?" he asked, reaching for the small bronze crescent in her open hand.

Olena offered the ring to him and Karl took it over to his work bench. He examined it with his tools while Olena explored the rest of his one room house.

On another table, she found a book that appeared to be about the many obelisks around the city and across the Southern Valley. Olena could not read the foreign writing, but she thought the pictures looked interesting. One showed the sun's rays reaching down from the sky to become the obelisks. Another page showed beams of light shooting out of the obelisks toward what seemed to be an attacking army.

"Can you feel their vibration," Karl asked without turning to see what she was doing.

Olena felt guilty for digging through his things. She did not understand what he asked her.

Karl turned toward her. "The obelisks. When someone with your power gets close enough, you should be able to feel the vibrations from their energy," he said.

"Oh, yes." Olena remembered the warm feeling she got. She also remembered that no one else seemed to notice it.

"I haven't quite got them figured out yet, but give me time and I will know their purpose," Karl said. "Now, tell me more about this ring and how it changes your appearance."

Olena told Karl about the Inhabitants. She explained that she could still see what happened outside when she was inside the ring. At least, that is how she thought of it. Olena imagined it was more likely that the bronze room existed inside the ring instead of somewhere far away.

She had a hard time concentrating because she wanted to play with all of the things that appeared to be toys in Karl's house. His inventions and devices seemed to be very fun, although she could not determine a purpose for any of them. If they worked, Olena guessed they would make a lot of movement and noise.

One particular piece caught her attention. It had a circular base about as wide as her hand. She counted ten pieces of metal sticking up from the edges that looked like tiny sails from a pirate ship.

"What does this do?" asked Olena.

"Nothing."

The answer disappointed her. "But it must do something. It looks fun."

"That is my problem. None of my creations ever work. I pride myself to be an inventor and alchemist. However, I am not successful with either. In fact, I am regularly and regrettably laughed out of the marketplace and have never been allowed in to see Queen Isis," explained Karl.

Olena felt bad for him. Karl seemed too nice. She wanted him to be successful even though she did not know him. She wished she could do something. With no better thought, she absently spun the circular invention.

"I'm doomed to be a failure," said Karl.

The device kept spinning after Olena took her hand away. She thought it appeared to be spinning faster. On their own, the sails shifted from pointing up to laying flat. The spinning object reminded Olena of her flying mayflower. The sails kept spinning like those giant petals. Then like her mayflower, Karl's creation lifted off the table.

"Doomed until now," Karl corrected himself. "What did you do?"

"Nothing. I only touched it. I'm sorry." Olena thought she might have done something wrong.

"Quick, touch something else," exclaimed Karl.

Olena moved about the room, putting her hands on every contraption she could see. Her excitement built with Karl's and he kept getting more and more excited. Soon flying, singing, crawling, ringing inventions filled the room. Instead of being angry, Karl must be thrilled to see his work come alive, she thought.

"Do you know what this means?" asked Karl. He put his hands on Olena's shoulders to hold her still, and then he picked her up in a great hug. "We work!"

"You mean, they work." Olena tried to correct him as he swung her about in his arms.

Karl gently set her down on a big cushion. He knelt to match her height. "No, I meant we work. You and I together work. My best ideas were nothing without your magic."

This sentence knocked the breath out of Olena. She did not realize she had been using her magic. For too long she had been trying too hard. Now without thinking, it happened.

"We work!" shouted Olena. The relief of her magic working almost made her cry.

She wanted to user her magic on something else. Olena knocked a large cushion out of her way to find something else. The sight behind it terrified her.

She stared into the face of a Rockhorn. The giant stone monsters almost destroyed Castle Empyrean and she did not even notice one buried under some pillows in the corner of Karl's small house.

Olena only had a moment to see the club and spike that served as its hands before Kez yelled, "Run!"

Olena did not quite make it to the door when Karl stopped her. He said, "You're not going anywhere."

Olena did not think he was bad, but maybe she was wrong. In the short time she had known him, she did not believe Karl would hurt her.

He said, "Wait, it's not alive."

Olena turned back to get another look at the Rockhorn. She stared in shock.

It had not moved. She suspected a real Rockhorn would have attacked her by now.

"I bought this off a guy that fought in that battle. He and some friends dragged it all the way back here as a trophy. When his wife saw it in her living room, she did not allow him to keep it. I've been trying for a year, but haven't been able to reanimate it," explained Karl.

The carved face stared back at her menacingly. She felt bad for thinking Karl had been trying to trap her, but even a lifeless Rockhorn still scared Olena. She studied its face. The small spikes circling its head looked like a sort of crown. It also had deep grooves all over its body inlayed with gold. If Olena did not know these things were evil, she could easily mistake it for a royal treasure. The stone legs, as wide as her body, looked uncomfortably folded beneath it. Olena wondered what would happen if she touched it.

"Do it," said Karl.

She thought for a moment that Karl could read her mind. Then Olena decided he was as curious as her. However, she thought not touching the monster would be the better choice. She did not want a Rockhorn rampaging through Hierakonpolis.

Karl moved closer and tripped again. He toppled to his hands and knees. Olena could not believe how clumsy he was. This time, though, he tripped over Sylvan, who had been left to dodge the wildly moving toys on the floor. Luckily for him, many of them were already dying down.

"Sorry about that, little fellow," apologized Karl. He made himself comfortable on the ground.

While sitting on the floor, Karl picked up Sylvan. He adjusted his glasses and then his eyes got wide.

Karl said, "I have an idea."

Chapter 12

At first, Olena did not like Karl's idea. At first, it seemed like a really bad idea.

Regardless of Olena's concern, the boy inventor set to work on the Rockhorn. He used a hammer and chisel to carve out a shallow cube in the Rockhorn's stomach.

After that, Karl searched his tables for a small jar of black ink. He dipped his finger in the ink and painted strange symbols inside the newly carved hole. The stains on his fingernails told Olena this must be his preferred way of writing and painting.

"What are you doing now?" she asked.

"Alchemy," came Karl's one word response.

Olena remembered the northern dwarves used alchemy. She did not understand it completely, but thought it was some kind of magic. She knew the dwarves used alchemy to make the new drawbridge at Castle Empyrean. Somehow, they combined fireproof Vexwood with the extra strong Greatwood to replace the one destroyed at the time of the Rockhorn Battle.

"So, you need my magic to make your alchemy work?" guessed Olena.

"It would be appreciated," said Karl.

She truly did not want to bring a Rockhorn to life, until she realized Karl's full plan. While she stood looking at the Rockhorn, Karl picked up Sylvan and whispered something to him.

Olena did not like Karl's idea, but Sylvan seemed open to it. Sylvan responded aloud, "Interesting. I would be willing to try."

Olena watched Karl place Sylvan in the carved hole in the Rockhorn's stomach. Sylvan fit perfectly, with almost no room to spare on the top or sides. The wooden man stuck out his arms and legs to firmly hold himself in place. An arm went in each corner above and he angled his legs into each corner at the bottom of the rectangular space. He looked like a letter X carved into the Rockhorn's stomach.

"If you would please, Your Majesty." Karl gestured for Olena to put her hand on the Rockhorn.

Reluctantly, Olena stepped forward. She carefully rested her fingertips on the Rockhorn's shoulder.

Nothing happened.

Olena expected as much. She figured it was one thing to animate small toys, but this was something else, something bigger.

Then Olena felt a shock. Some small amount of energy passed from her to the stone giant. This jolt stung her fingers. Olena heard a minute tapping sound, like pebbles rolling down off the Rockhorn. The giant quickly stood up and she expected it to attack.

Instead, it stretched its arms and waved them slowly back and forth in front of its carved face. Could Sylvan really be controlling it, Olena wondered. Then, at its full height, the Rockhorn's head scraped the ceiling.

Olena asked, "Sylvan, is that you?"

The Rockhorn took a bow, but Sylvan did not speak.

"An unfortunate side effect," said Karl. "The binding must have rendered him speechless."

The Sylvan-Rockhorn nodded in agreement.

Even though Sylvan's high-pitched voice sometimes hurt her ears, Olena did not want her friend to lose the ability to talk.

"You don't have to stay like that. We can take you out of there," she said.

Sylvan shook his giant stone head from side to side meaning no. She thought he must like his new size. Olena also noticed his wooden body did not move at all now that he connected to the Rockhorn.

Sylvan stood patiently with his weapon shaped hands on his hips. Kez climbed up and hung from his tail on Sylvan's left arm. He dangled near the Rockhorn's midsection, apparently thinking that Sylvan could still hear him through his wooden body.

"Do you feel alright?" he asked.

Sylvan raised his left arm, bringing Kez with it. He deposited the quzzak on his shoulder.

"So you use this head to hear?" asked Kez.

Sylvan nodded.

"And see?" added Olena.

Sylvan nodded again. He began walking around the room. The horns on his head left little grooves in the stone ceiling. Sylvan's new size and coordination impressed Olena. While he gave his display, Olena noticed Karl packing books and devices. Most things he stuffed into a large sack, but a few things that seemed important to him went into a smaller pouch.

When he finished, Karl said, "I think we have everything we need. Books, check. Giant bodyguard, check. Magic ring, check."

With the excitement of using her own magic, Olena almost forgot about the Bronze Ring. She slipped her hand into her pocket to find the ring resting safely. Now that she touched it again, she felt the urge to wear it.

Olena quickly decided she did not want to do that. What if she became trapped again, she asked herself. She felt like she got to know Ovara pretty well, but the girl still seemed like she was hiding something. Worse still, what if one of the other Inhabitants that she knew nothing about got free?

Karl must have noticed the troubled look on her face. He said, "You do have the ring? I'm sure

I gave it back to you before we started working on your wooden friend."

"It's here," Olena said, patting her pocket. "I'm not going to put it on though."

"Your choice," said Karl. Then he pulled a small circular object from his front vest pocket. Holding it by its thin chain, he flipped open the metal lid and looked inside. Then he dipped it back out of sight.

"What was that?" asked Olena.

"A pocket watch. They're very popular in the west," answered Karl without more explanation. Olena never heard of such a thing and could not imagine a use for it.

He slung the pouch over his shoulder by its strap. Then he hoisted the large bag onto his back.

"It tells us that it's time to go," Karl said.

Olena mused that she never had to keep track of time in Banookanook.

Before Karl could take his first step, the weight of the bag toppled him backwards. Olena quickly helped him to his feet.

"On second thought, it would be more prudent to leave this here. I don't think we'll need any of that where we're going." Karl left the over-stuffed bag on the floor where he fell.

Olena found herself constantly amused by this boy. He knew things he should not and apparently had whole conversations in his head, which he sometimes shared part of with the outside world. During this particular conversation, he decided they needed to go somewhere and assumed everyone else would come with him.

"Where are we going?" asked Kez, from what appeared to be his new favorite spot high atop Sylvan's Rockhorn shoulder.

For whatever reason Ovara decided to bring Kez and Sylvan on this journey, it made Olena feel safe to have them with her. Both of them always watched out for her. She would have asked Karl about his plans. Still, Kez did his best to protect her and usually asked those important questions before she could.

Karl stopped. He pursed his lips and stared at the door. Maybe he forgot where he wanted to go, thought Olena. Then he strained his face like he was trying to make a hard decision.

Finally, he said, "Ah. We have to go see a friend of yours. I'm sorry, but we must. No arguments."

"That's fine," said Olena, "but what friend could I possibly have here?"

"The Queen of the Southern Valley, of course," said Karl.

This plan excited Olena. It also made her slightly nervous. Maybe being near the queen would be a good thing, but she thought she might be in trouble for sneaking out of Castle Empyrean. If she had a chance to explain that she did not really do it and she could show Ovara to Queen Isis, she might not be in trouble. Then she remembered she did not really want to put the ring on again.

Sylvan, with Kez on his shoulder, already squeezed out the front door. With Karl following behind them, it appeared there would be no further discussion about their destination. Olena took one more look around the jumbled mess that Karl Lumpkin called home. All but a few of his creations finally wound down. She left the room quiet and still. On the way out the door, she noticed some writing that she could read surrounded by other pictures and unusual symbols. Karl must use the walls to make notes, she thought. This one looked like an important reminder.

Note to Self:

Self,

it is your duty to protect the Last Queen No Matter What, No Matter When, No Matter Why. P.S. Don't Let Her read this.

Olena did not like the sound of that note. It could mean too many things and none of them good. Olena did not want to ask Karl about it. She wished she never read it. Olena quickly joined the others in the alley and pretended she did not see the ominous message.

Karl led them out to the main street. With two easy turns, they mingled into a crowded street. For some reason, it seemed easier to leave Karl's house than it was to find it.

No one on the avenue seemed to mind the Rockhorn walking among them. Why does it not scare them, wondered Olena. She sometimes had nightmares about the Rockhorns and she only saw one close up after it had been defeated in the battle. Could people forget about something so horrible after only a year?

In any case, no one bothered them, so they made their way through the city. With each turn onto a wider, more crowded street, Olena had the sense they were being followed. She had no proof however. Each time she looked behind her, she could see no one looking at them. Even feeling protected, her anxiety must be getting the better of her.

The last time she turned around, Karl said, "Did you see them?"

This convinced Olena. It gave her some relief, but it was replaced by the fear of confirmation that they were being followed. She whispered to Karl, "I don't see anyone, but I know they're back there."

"Two jackals, about a hundred feet back," said Karl.

Olena tried to look.

"Don't look," Karl said with urgency.

Olena explained, "I thought I saw two jackals following us to your house earlier. What do you think they want?"

"You, I'm sure."

Karl's answer did not make her feel good.

"Then who do they work for?" she asked.

"Let's ask them," said Karl, "if you feel like begging."

"What kind of answer is that?" asked Olena. Karl's eccentricities frustrated her at the moment.

"The best one I have," said Karl. He grabbed her by the arm and pulled her behind a statue of a lion with a human head. This statue reminded her of the Alkonosts. Those beautiful creatures had the bodies of birds and heads of women. She saw them once or twice at the Palace by the Sea. Sadly, the Forgotten Evil destroyed the last two in existence during the attack on the previous Queen of the Eastern Sky.

They waited for what felt like an incredibly long time. Finally, the jackals walked past them. They kept going without looking back or trying to find their prey.

"Maybe they weren't following us," said Olena.

As soon as she said that, two different jackal-headed men appeared around the corner. Both with swords drawn, they charged at Olena.

Sylvan stepped in between them and with one swing of his clubbed hand, knocked their swords away. The jackals turned their attack on Sylvan. They hit and bit him, but it seemed to have no effect on his stone body. Sylvan smacked one of them to the ground, unconscious. He pinned the other to the wall with his pointed spear-like left hand.

"Who do you work for?" demanded Kez.

The jackal did not answer. Sylvan pressed his dangerous hand harder to the jackal's chest.

"Who?" asked Kez again.

"We serve," started the jackal man. Then the other jackal regained consciousness. He threw his sword into the pinned jackal, ending his confession. Then the surviving jackal ran off into the crowd.

"Don't let him get away," shouted Kez.

Sylvan started to follow, but Karl stopped him by saying, "It's too late. We'll be safely in the Infinity Temple before he can bring back any friends."

Now Olena did not care about being in trouble for running away. She did not want to be on these unsafe streets any longer. If Isis got mad at her that would be better than being captured by jackals, or worse.

Karl led them the rest of the way to the Infinity Temple. Before long, they stood at the gates in the center of Hierakonpolis.

Olena looked at the massive temple that stretched into the distance as far as she could see. Another pyramid rose up in the center of the temple compound.

"Now I know why they call it the Infinity Temple," she said. "It's huge."

"Actually," Karl corrected, "inside the main temple, there are catacombs and other rooms that go on forever. In times of danger, the queen can retreat to one of these rooms. If an enemy made it inside, they would become lost forever in the catacombs."

Somehow, this did not make the temple seem any safer to Olena. At either side of the gate, the guards with snake heads did not make her feel any more welcome either. Their heads were wider than the other snake people she had seen. Karl identified them as cobras. They also had intricate designs painted on the back of their scaly hoods. This meant they were royal guards, hand chosen by the queen, he explained.

"Identify yoursssssself," hissed the head guard.

Karl said, "May I present Olena the Beautiful, Queen of the Eastern Sky."

The cobra men talked in a private huddle. After a moment, they agreed to let Olena and her friends into the temple.

Inside, Olena marveled at the wide courtyard. The walls seemed much taller than they did from outside. Each stone looked precisely cut and laid exactly in place. The tiles beneath their feet looked the same.

A catwoman hurried out the closing gate, otherwise this courtyard was empty. At the far end, two identical statues flanked a wide archway. Both statues represented a beautiful young woman holding the sun above her head. Olena thought the sun disk looked like it was made from real gold.

"She was the first Queen of the Southern Valley," offered Karl.

They made their way across the courtyard. Between the statues, the archway led to a short flight of stairs. At the top of the stairs, the archway opened onto another courtyard. This one did not look quite as big as the first. However, there were more statues here.

These statues looked like the original animals with which many of the Hierakonpolitans shared their faces. Olena recognized the hippopotamus with a small crocodile on its back. Also, she saw one that looked exactly like the hawkman, Horus, which they met in the marketplace. Another figure looked like a giant bull. Olena knew this was supposed to be Apis. She never met Apis, but she remembered him being one of the heroes of the Rockhorn Battle.

This made Olena feel sad for all the people and animals they lost that day. She had not thought about the battle in a long time. Now with Sylvan using the body of a Rockhorn and seeing the statue of Apis, the memories came back to her. She remembered Isis told her Apis would be reincarnated. Knowing Apis could be born again made her feel somewhat better about the loss.

"Welcome to the Infinity Temple," said a warm, comforting voice.

Olena looked around to see who said that. She saw no people, but in the next archway, she spotted a black cat.

As they approached, Olena asked, "Can you talk?"

"Should I not?" replied the cat. He flicked his tail back and forth.

Being the first actual cat Olena saw in the south, it surprised her that he could talk. She had only recently gotten used to seeing people with cat heads and tails. A real cat seemed unusual.

"So, we are welcome here?" asked Karl.

"Naturally," said the black cat.

"Then can we come in?" asked Karl.

The cat stood up on all four legs, looking annoyed as most cats usually do. He arched his back in a great stretch that ended in his tail.

"Follow me," he said. "Queen Isis is waiting for you."

As they walked along the narrow, torch-lit corridors, Olena stared at the continuous wall paintings. They seemed to tell the entire history of the Southern Valley. Olena thought she recognized things like Castle Empyrean and a black shape that must have been the Forgotten Evil being defeated by the First Queen. The images had to be thousands of years old, but the smooth walls almost shined like the paint was brand new.

"What should we call you?" Kez politely asked from Sylvan's shoulder. Always the ambassador, Olena liked that Kez tried to make friends wherever he went.

To her surprise, the cat responded, "You may call me Apis."

Chapter 13

Y ou're a legend," Karl said to Apis, as they followed him down the hall. "I thought you'd be bigger."

"Amusing," replied Apis. "I thought you'd be smarter than to say something like that. Size does not determine power."

This seemed both like a threat and a message to Olena. She did not think Apis really meant to threaten them. Maybe because he was a giant bull for so long, it frustrated him to now be a cat. Also, she wondered if the message was intended for her. She doubted her own power because she was only a little girl.

The idea of Apis still being powerful made Olena curious. She asked, "What happened to you?"

"It has been my privilege to serve with the Queen of the Southern Valley since the beginning. With the passage of time, it becomes necessary for me to leave my body and start over with a new one," explained Apis.

"But aren't you supposed to be a bull?" asked Kez.

"That is something I do not understand. Normally, I do return to my bovine form. This is the first time out of nine that I have come back as a feline."

Olena had a feeling and said, "Do you think it has to do with the Forgotten Evil?"

"In my best estimation, that may be the answer," said Apis. "Although we stopped his return a year ago, somehow I have been affected."

Karl said, "Maybe he tried to restrict your power by forcing you into a smaller form? There have been more followers of the Forgotten Evil making themselves known. They may still be trying to revive him."

"That makes the most sense," said the cat. After that, Apis did not speak for a while.

Continuing down the hall, Olena studied the intricate paintings. She noticed how every corner of tile had been precisely laid. The torches seemed to be spaced too far apart and many of the side halls were completely dark.

Although the temple was darker than she would have liked, it felt safe.

Feeling safe had become quite important to Olena over the past year. Until the day she met her mother, she had not thought about it much. When she lost the woman that she only dreamt about before, it awoke something in her. Of course, her adventure to Castle Empyrean had plenty of scary moments. However, the brief instant that she hugged her lost mother made her greatly feel the need for comfort and security.

They passed several more intersections, but saw no one until they entered the main chamber. Isis sat on her stone throne. It looked, to Olena, as if it was carved out of one giant rock into a perfectly square seat with wide arm rests. Four cat-headed women attended the queen, two on each side of her.

"I expected this day would come," said Queen Isis.

"Forgive me, Your Majesty. It's my fault," started Kez.

Isis stood and, using her sistrum-cane, moved over to them.

Olena spoke up, "It's not. It's my fault. I had to get out of there."

Isis put her long, wrinkled fingers under Olena's chin and tilted her head upward so they could look in each other's eyes.

"We only did it to protect you. We thought keeping you isolated at Castle Empyrean would keep you safe from our changing world," said

Isis. "It is understandable that you would feel the need to be free."

She did not seem upset at all, thought Olena. She asked, "You're not mad?"

"Oh, I am quite disappointed," said Isis. "Alas, you are here now and we must deal with that."

"Begging your pardon, but there are several things we need to deal with," said Karl.

Isis turned her intense gaze on Karl. "I see you are still up to your old tricks," Isis said, gesturing at the Rockhorn form of Sylvan.

"I never stop," said Karl, proudly.

"With that truth, Mr. Lumpkin, your reputation precedes you," said the old queen. "I hope you haven't caused too many disasters in my marketplace lately."

"None that I couldn't walk away from," smiled Karl.

Queen Isis said, "To business then. What are your other items we need to deal with?"

Karl nudged Olena forward. He said, "We, uh, ran into some friends on the way here."

"Two jackals attacked us," added Olena. "I think they were following me, but I was in disguise."

"Disguise or not," said Isis, "with enough dark magic, we can be identified. Did they say anything?"

"Nothing to give us any clue toward their intent, but only one got away," said Kez.

"It is likely they followed her since she entered the city," said Karl. "Definitely from the marketplace to my house."

"The marketplace," exclaimed Olena. "Maybe that's where they came from. We met a man in the marketplace."

"A man with a hawk's head," corrected Kez.

Olena agreed, "Right. Horus. He had a message for you, but was afraid to deliver it in person. He said Emperor Li-Am is the leader of the Arcosaurans, but they are not all bad."

"Arcosaurans, you say?" asked Isis. "A favorite bedtime story of southern children."

Karl looked surprised. He said to Olena, "You didn't tell me that. The Arcosaurans aren't real. They can't be, not anymore."

"Mr. Lumpkin, you know as well as I that Horus does not provide incorrect information," said Isis. "It's about time we can put a name to our troublesome neighbors."

Olena whispered to Karl, "What's wrong with Arcosaurans?"

"Nothing, if you don't mind ferocious monsters in league with the Forgotten Evil."

These Arcosaurans sounded like trouble, thought Olena. First, they block the Brygos from flowing, and then they threaten the borders of the Southern Valley. Besides that, they had something that seemed very important to Captain Aeran and his fellow Guardian Hawks.

"Can you tell me more about the problems with the Arcosaurans?" Olena asked Isis.

The old queen had to rest her tired body and sat back on her throne.

Queen Isis said, "It is an old story, yet very short. It has been said Empyrean began with a war and will end with a war. In the First War for Empyrean, the Arcosaurans fought alongside the Forgotten Evil. After his defeat, they vanished. It makes sense now that they retreated to the far south. Perhaps it took them some time to reorganize, but eventually, they took control of the Brygos. That put a stranglehold on our land."

"Why have you tolerated it for so long?" asked Kez.

"For peace," answered Isis. "While the Southern Valley does not thrive like it did under the previous queens, we still survive. Now, the strangers demand more of our land beyond the Unending Desert. That would give them control over Hierakonpolis and some of our most fertile farms."

"Sounds like an invasion to me," said Karl.

Isis said, "I fear you are not far off. Olena, we queens have tried to shield you from this. However, after the attack on Castle Empyrean and the incident with your mother, this may mark the beginnings of the Second War for Empyrean. Because you have thrust yourself into these events, I tell you this now."

Karl added, "With the Arcosaurans and whoever the jackals work for, it sounds like you have plenty of enemies."

"I do not wish to sound so negative," said Kez, "but do not forget about Sasha and General Gusk. Neither of them was found after the Rockhorn Battle either. Because Vanril survived the battle, we have to assume they survived too."

Olena remembered both the gypsy witch and the snail-like creature known as General Gusk. Along with the dwarf lord Vanril, they orchestrated the attack that led to Olena becoming queen. Her friend William stopped Vanril, which led to the restoration of the Dead Forest. However, while hunting continued still, no one could find Sasha or Gusk, if they were in hiding.

Then Olena thought about Raymond Shaydaway. She remembered Zandria saying the man who trapped their mother confessed to being a servant of the Forgotten Evil too. Now this Emperor Li-Am is starting an invasion of the Southern Valley. Olena wondered how many more servants were still in hiding. She feared soon, nowhere would be safe.

Isis stood again. The decorative metal sistrum on her cane jingled as she moved. She said, "All things will come to pass. As it is, I want you all dressed in your finest for a banquet. In the morning, I will send word to Empyrean that you are safe with me. Tonight, we dine with the Emperor's ambassador, his human ambassador. At least knowing who this man serves may give us the upper hand."

The catwomen led Olena and Karl to separate rooms, where they bathed and dressed. Olena chose a purple silk robe, her favorite color. Two of the handmaids worked for thirty minutes trying to flatten Olena's hair into a traditional southern hairstyle. Eventually, like all before them, they surrendered to the curls.

When she finally made it to the dining room, everyone else sat, waiting for her. Olena liked Karl's simple outfit of a shirt and pants, tied at the waist with a sash, much like Ovara's. He must really like his vest, but it did not match his new clothes, although he still wore it. And apparently due to his clumsiness, he already had a food stain on his shirt and tussled hair.

Another man Olena did not know sat next to Queen Isis. The sight of him gave her goose bumps. His gross, wart-covered face looked twisted in pain. Maybe he had an upset stomach, thought Olena. He wore dull brown robes that did not cover his wooden leg sticking out past the end of the table. Olena also noticed a small snake wrapped around his wrist like a living bracelet. She saw a few people back at the marketplace with similar jewelry.

"May I present Spynum Begg," said Isis.

Olena curtseyed like Cinderella had taught her. Spynum Begg did not return any gesture of greeting. He only seemed interested in eating and talking business with Isis.

Olena did not see Kez or Sylvan anywhere. Karl explained that they would not be joining them at Spynum Begg's request. He apparently wanted a private audience in order to have both queens' full attention. The queen arranged for Kez to eat with the servants while Sylvan opted to wait back in Olena's room. Then after the food was served, the handmaidens left the four of them alone. Karl and Olena sat at the far end of the table while Isis and Begg discussed the border issue. Olena could not hear most of the conversation until Isis became upset. She wondered why she and Karl were even there.

"You can tell Emperor Li-Am that we are not afraid of him," said the Queen of the Southern Valley.

Begg looked momentarily surprised, then angry. He said, "So, you know my master. Then there is nothing more to hide, but I do have one final duty."

In horror, Olena watched Begg unravel the snake from his wrist. He ran his gnarled hand along its short body and the snake grew stiff, as if in a trance. He held it by its tail and Olena thought it now looked like a dagger. And like a dagger, Spynum Begg stabbed Queen Isis with it.

"No!" screamed Olena.

"Get out of here," ordered Karl, shoving Olena from her chair.

She could not run at first. She watched Isis' lifeless body hit the floor. As soon as the old queen lay still, the stiff snake loosened and slithered away. Begg turned on Olena.

"I did not expect an opportunity for two queens," he said as he hobbled toward her. "My jackals may have failed, but I won't."

Karl pushed her again as he said, "Run!"

This time, Olena ran. She did not know where to go and could barely see in the torch-lit halls with streaming tears in her eyes. She turned corners as fast as she could. Eventually, she found herself back in the dining room. She saw Isis' unmoving body. Not far from that, Karl lay on the floor, his cracked glasses landed in a plate of food, apparently knocked from his face. He did not move either.

Then Spynum Begg entered behind her. He looked sweaty from running. Olena did not have time to check on either of her friends or even call for help. She dashed out another door.

When Olena turned the last corner, she tumbled down a flight of steps into total darkness. It took her a moment to recover. When she looked up the stairs, toward the light, she could see the grotesque shape of Spynum Begg coming down the stairs. Olena ran screaming into the blackness.

The dark halls seemed to go on forever. After a while, her throat hurt and her feet hurt. She could not scream any longer. She could not cry any longer. And she could not run any longer.

Olena did not think stopping was an option, so she crept on in the darkness. She guessed she must be in the catacombs that Karl told her about. Poor Karl, she thought. Then she thought about Isis. How could she be so careless? Olena hoped she would make it out of this maze. If she did, she would use all of her power to stop Spynum Begg and his master, Li-Am.

Somewhere in the dark, after Olena caught her breath, she heard something. The noise came at her low, like something skittering across the floor. With the countless turns and intersections, she guessed the crunchy noise could be echoing from anywhere. Crunchy? Was that how she would describe it, Olena wondered. Yes, she decided, crunchy, like when they walked on the dry leaves of the Dead Forest.

"What does it matter?" she whispered. "I can't see anything anyway. It could be right in front of me."

Then Olena did see something right in front of her. A small gold circle of light appeared, probably from around a corner. It stopped as if it saw her. The circle seemed so bright in the pitch black. As quickly as it appeared, the circle disappeared.

Olena tried to follow and felt her way around a corner. There, two more of the things waited for her. Now three bright gold circles of light moved across the floor. As she stepped close, they moved away, making that crunchy sound as they went.

The creatures, she assumed they were creatures, led her down the hall. She hoped they were leading her away from Spynum Begg. When she came to a wide room lit by only a few torches, she knew Begg had to be waiting for her. Plain sandstone columns dissected the room, casting long shadows in every direction from the wavering torches.

No jackals jumped out at her and she did not find Spynum Begg. She did find that the gold circles were bugs. As they passed from shadow to light, Olena could see they were about as big as her fist with intricate patterns on their backs and two long pincers sticking out in front. She remembered Isis once wearing a necklace that looked like this. The Queen of the Southern Valley called it a scarab.

For some reason, the scarabs bolted out of sight. However, Olena did not feel alone. Something moved behind one of the pillars to her right. The low-ceilinged room suddenly felt very small as she noticed movement on her left too.

"Ughhhhhmmmmm....." came the sound from behind the pillars, in the darkest parts of the room.

Olena did not like the low moaning that came out of the shadows. She wanted to run, but did not think being in the dark catacombs would be an improvement. Whatever dwelt in this room, it was coming out to meet her.

The weak torch light outlined a slow-moving figure. As it cleared the last pillar into the open center of the room, Olena could see it. The man looked ancient. The skin on his face peeled off in dry, dusty flakes. Brown, tattered strips of cloth that used to be white wrapped his entire body. The second figure, looking almost the same, stumbled forward with his arms sticking straight out. These things, that used to be men, did not seem very friendly. Olena wondered how long they had been waiting down here. Then she wondered if they were waiting for her.

They kept creeping slowly toward her and always moaning. By the time Olena counted four of the bandaged figures, she could not take it any longer. For the second time that night, she ran into the black tunnels screaming.

Eventually, Olena came to a dead end. She still could not see anything, not even the scarabs, but could feel walls on three sides of her. If Begg caught up to her now, she could do nothing. She did not know if that would be worse than the dry old men.

Then, Olena thought of the Walking Portal. She knew it was supposed to help her in times of emergency. She quickly tried it, but nothing happened. This is a terrible time for her magic not to work, she thought. She could not imagine that it might only work with Karl. Then she remembered Ovara could do the portal. She reached for the ring and realized she left it in the pocket of her other dress back in her room.

While she stood at the end of this hall, wondering how she would escape, no sound of moaning came to her. She expected to hear their shuffling feet or the step-tap of Spynum Begg chasing her in these black tunnels. Maybe someone captured him or maybe he escaped?

Either way, Olena did not think he was after her anymore.

She relaxed for a moment and leaned against the wall at the end of the hall. However, the wall did not support her. Instead, it slid back a few feet, and then rose up, opening onto a new passage.

Inside, Olena could see light. She could make out about ten steep steps that led up to the light. Olena could not imagine wandering back through the pitch black catacombs, so she went toward the light.

At the top of the stairs, Olena could see the source of the light. A small white pyramid, glowing from the inside, sat atop a short pillar. It looked to be right at her height. The pillar stood at the end of a walkway that appeared to be barely wide enough for her feet. On either side, she could see straight down into nothingness. She looked up and to the sides, only to see the same nothingness. The room appeared to be impossibly large, if it had walls at all.

"The Eternity Temple," said Olena. Her voice echoed in the emptiness and it startled her. She did not know how she knew the name of this room, but she did. Then she noticed hundreds of scarabs flying about the room. Some came close to light her way, while others fluttered off, disappearing in the immensity of the vast room.

The glowing pyramid seemed to call to her. Olena carefully stepped out onto the walkway.

She wanted to crawl for fear of falling. However, she made it to the pillar without a single misstep, thanks to the golden scarab light.

Olena started to put her hands on the pyramid, but changed her mind a moment before she touched it. It felt warm this close, maybe warm enough to burn her. Besides, the last time she touched something, she brought a Rockhorn back to life.

Now she stared at the small pyramid and immediately thought she understood its power. The Eternity Temple allowed her to see backward in time.

First, she saw Spynum Begg attack Isis and chase her. Instead of following her trail, the vision stayed in the dining room. She saw Karl try to stop Begg, but the man knocked Karl to the floor. She then watched herself come back to the dining room. This time, she noticed the gold dust forming on Isis that meant she was passing into the twilight. Right after she left, Karl awoke. He must only have been unconscious. Olena felt relieved for at least that. Then Karl got help from Kez and Sylvan. They led the cobra-headed guards into the catacombs.

It did no good. Olena saw Begg escape through a secret passage with the help of a jackal. She recognized this dog-headed man as the surviving attacker from earlier in the street. Behind the Infinity Temple, strange looking men riding on strange looking beasts waited for Begg. The lizard men in armor took off across the Unending Desert, heading south with Begg on their two-legged mounts.

After a moment, the images started moving faster and lasting shorter. She saw the day Zandria found her mother, then the day she became queen. Then the images became brief flashes.

One image confused her though. A woman, who might have been Zandria, stood next to a copper-haired man, who could only have been Adam. They looked older and possibly as if they were getting married.

Could the Eternity Temple show the future as well, Olena asked herself.

Then more images flooded her mind, moving almost too fast to comprehend. Before the white light overwhelmed her, she caught a glimpse of herself. She looked maybe four or five years old and she looked happy. She sat with Zandria, playing in the sand at the edge of the sea in Banookanook.

Olena started crying and closed her eyes. When she opened them, she found herself in a guest bedroom of the Infinity Temple. She had no idea how she made it back to her room, but Kez, Sylvan and Karl sat at her bedside.

She felt safe again, for now.

Chapter 14

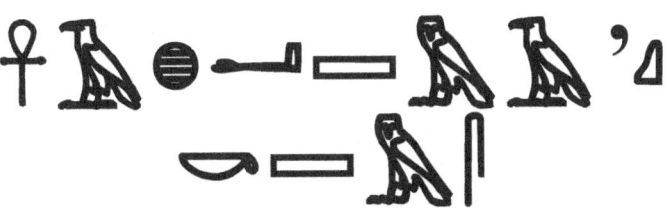

Zandria needed the trip back to Banookanook. Although she had traveled some since leaving home, she had purposely not gone all the way back there until now. She felt like she had a hole in her heart after losing both parents. Thinking of her old home seemed to make it bigger, but the warmth of Castle Empyrean filled it, mostly.

After helping her sister become queen and freeing her mother, Zandria felt lost. She wanted a direction or a purpose. For that reason, she decided to travel a lot with her new best friend, Dew. Usually, Adam would complete the trio.

Before coming back to see Olena, Zandria and her friends visited Soria Moria. She liked that Olena gave her a castle. What girl would not want her own castle, Zandria thought. She wished she did not have to wait another five or six years for the restoration to be complete. At least the craftsmen were already working on it.

The girls convinced Adam to lead them over the Euphoric Mountains by way of the secret pass. Zandria hoped they would see Evorin on their way back to Castle Empyrean. Sadly, they found the dragon nest empty. Even Dew did not know enough about the nearly extinct creatures to guess where he might have gone. No one had seen Evorin for almost a year now.

Zandria found her main joy on the long coach ride to Banookanook to be spending time with her sister. She truly loved the curly haired little girl and knew without a doubt she would do anything for her.

Unfortunately, Zandria could not say the same thing about the other queens. She believed they were wonderful, but none of them were her sister. In truth, spending so much time with them made her uncomfortable. She thought they secretly disliked her, but had no good reason why or any proof.

Olena's plans for a Palace on the Sea excited Zandria. She imagined she would want to spend as much time there as she would at Soria Moria. This made her think about living apart from her sister.

For the first six years of Olena's life, they had been each other's playmate, confidant and best friend. Suddenly, their whole world turned upside down. Zandria had new companions and Olena had new confidants. She wanted to believe they would always be close, but after only a year, Zandria could already feel their relationship changing.

On the final part of the journey, they met Wrath and his unicorn friend, Sayonya. The news of Cayomi's recovery made her happy. She believed rescuing Cayomi from Shaydaway's Carnivale Chaotica was one of the best things she had ever done. Somehow, it also made her realize that she felt trapped. She thought about the unicorns' freedom and wanted the same for herself. She had the feeling her sister wanted the same thing, but they never talked about it.

At least, Zandria had some of that freedom. Once they made certain that the four queens were safely returned to Castle Empyrean, Zandria, Dew and Adam went north.

"I didn't want to make a big deal of this," Dew said as they travelled the North Road, "but we are going to be home in time for my grandmother's two thousand and twentieth birthday."

"Did you say two thousand?" asked Adam.

"That would mean she is older than Empyrean," offered Kalis. He and Adam seemed to be almost as inseparable as Dew and Tihi.

"Right. She met the first queens," said Dew.

"That's amazing. I wonder what that was like?" asked Zandria.

"Probably not as interesting as you'd hope," said Dew.

Tihi said, "I doubt the party will be like the one twenty years ago."

"Some of the other clans should be there," said Dew. "But I wouldn't expect too much excitement though."

Zandria soon discovered Dew's prediction was correct. Mostly, the elves paid tribute to Dew's grandmother, Malika Lantisphere. They met with her one at a time or in pairs, but not more than that. They sat away from everyone else and spoke quietly. Everyone ate well, but had no singing or story-telling like Zandria remembered from her first visit to Truewood Forest.

It did give Zandria time to work on her archery. Over the past several months, Dew had been teaching her to use a bow and arrow.

"This is your most important weapon," Dew reminded her.

"Because it is silent and can keep your target at a distance," Zandria said. Dew told her this every time they practiced. Still, Zandria appreciated Dew's expertise. With her help, Zandria could now hit a bull's-eye from Tihi's back while galloping.

One night, while they ate with some of the Algis Clan, something interrupted their meal. Zandria wanted to hear about the Algis family and their travels in the frozen north, but the two elves stopped talking in mid-sentence. Zandria looked around the camp. She saw every elf, including Dew, sat completely motionless. They seemed to be listening to something.

"What is it?" whispered Zandria.

Hiemal Algis, the northern clan leader, gently hushed her. Then he pointed west, into the dark forest.

Suddenly, a black bird swooped out of the night. Zandria thought it looked big enough to pick her up and it looked angry. Then two more of the furious birds flew into the camp.

"The Ravens," shouted Dew.

Elves dashed for their weapons as four more of the ravens appeared. The camp became chaos. Zandria only counted seven ravens, but they attacked like an army. Too many elves received injuries from beak and claw.

One of the ravens turned on Zandria. A moment before its claws reached her hair, Dew stopped it with a precisely aimed arrow. The large bird dropped to the ground.

The whole incident lasted only a few minutes. Unfortunately, the elf clans lost almost twenty family members before they defeated the ravens. Even Malika suffered a severe injury.

"What were those things?" asked Adam.

Dew explained, "The Seven Ravens. A few hundred years ago, they were human brothers, but their father cursed them. They were lazy and disobedient, so he turned them into ravens as punishment. The brothers' behavior only worsened and the old man never had the chance to turn them back. This is the first time in my life that they dared venture outside of Peckwood Forest."

Hiemal approached, pulling on his thick white fur coat. Zandria wondered what animal that fur came from. It looked magnificent. Hiemal said, "Things are not right in Truewood. The Algis Clan is returning to the far north tonight."

"We could use you here," said Dew. "The problem is not only in our forest. All of Empyrean is changing." Dew turned to Zandria and it made her feel uncomfortable. She said, "This raven attack is only a symptom. Don't let the queens fool you. Too many bad things are happening these days."

"Like Olena not being able to use her powers?" asked Zandria.

"That and more. Maybe you sent the Forgotten Evil back into the bottomless pit, but he is not defeated. His followers are on the rise," said Dew.

Zandria noticed all of the elves looked concerned and maybe a little frightened by this thought. Only Dew's grandmother, Malika, did not look scared. Zandria already had a difficult time understanding Malika because she only spoke elven and she could not read her ancient, wrinkled face. The fresh bandage covering her injured eye made it more difficult.

For the first time in Zandria's experience, Malika spoke so she could understand. The old elf said, "The darkness is returning."

That night, Zandria barely slept. She kept expecting more ravens to attack, or maybe some curses. What if a pack of werewolves found them, she wondered. Zandria had Tihi saddled at dawn. She wanted to get back to Castle Empyrean. At least, she thought, she would feel a little safer there than out in a forest.

"I'm staying," said Dew. "The other clans went home during the night and my grandmother needs me. There are not many of us left in True Wood."

"I understand," said Zandria.

Dew said, "Please tell Tym what happened. Also, tell the queens that they may not be able to count on all elves, but the Lantisphere Clan will support them in what's to come."

Tihi requested to stay with Dew, so Zandria rode behind Adam on Kalis. Although they travelled alone, nothing happened on the long trip back to Castle Empyrean.

They returned to find the castle in an uproar. Fury met them in the courtyard.

"I'm sorry to be the one to tell you this, but I thought it should come from a friend first," said the Friesian General. "Olena is missing."

Zandria felt her breath stop as if someone hit her in the chest. Too many unpleasant thoughts tore through her mind. Especially after the attack in Truewood Forest, she could only think the worst.

"What happened?" demanded Adam.

"It will be best to discuss it with the other two queens inside," said Fury.

Zandria could not bring herself to speak, but she noticed Fury said two queens.

Apparently, Adam noticed it too. He said, "Two queens? What's happening here?"

"Isis had to return to the Southern Valley. Don't worry. Tym will take you to the queens and they will explain everything," said Fury.

The elven butler waited at the top of the six glass steps that led into the crystal castle. Zandria could not imagine losing her sister and this paralyzed her. Adam had to pull her by her hand as they navigated the magically changing hallways of the castle.

Tym Lantisphere led them to Queen Snow White and Queen Cinderella. Besides the elderly queens, several Empyrical Wizards sat around the massive dining table along with William, Aleta and Eisenhahn, the iron-skinned giant.

As soon as they entered, William came to Zandria and knelt in front of her. Still in shock, Zandria did not know what he was doing.

"Please forgive me," he said.

"What?" said Zandria. She had too many questions, but could only manage that one word.

"It's my fault," continued William. "I should have been here to protect her, not touring the countryside like a love struck youth."

Zandria did notice Aleta looked slightly embarrassed by his words. Still, she felt the southern woman liked the idea of William being in love with her. This thought distracted

Zandria for a fraction of a moment before the Queen of the Northern Wood spoke.

"We do not believe she is in any danger," said Snow White. "We are embarrassed to admit that we believe she ran away."

The words slipped out before Zandria could stop herself, "I don't blame her."

William looked a little shocked and had to hide a smile. Luckily for Zandria, no one else heard her or at least they pretended like they did not.

Zandria started to become calm. She knew nothing could harm the queens inside the castle. Besides, she believed if it was serious, they would have sent someone for her immediately.

Cinderella offered, "Both Kez and Sylvan are gone, as well. The three of them have gone off together somewhere like irresponsible children."

"My sister is not irresponsible." This time Zandria spoke loud enough to be clearly heard by everyone in the room. She wanted to be heard. "She's worked hard for a year trying to please you. She wants to be a good queen in memory of our mother and for all of Empyrean. Things are changing in our world and you've kept her locked in this tower because you're scared. She is still a kid though."

Snow White stood, her flowing white hair draped over her shoulders. Zandria could not remember when her hair turned from midnight black to white. She thought it was strange for a woman so old to have black hair in the first place. Now, it only served as another reminder of the older queens' weakening power. Snow White came forward and Zandria anticipated a stern response.

Instead, the Queen of the Northern Wood said, "You are right. We have been pushing her hard because of the troubling changes. We do still fear that the Forgotten Evil may return. That is why we must not fail in keeping Olena safe."

Zandria liked the idea of being right, especially in front of the queens. She felt like she could never be good enough for them any other time. She never told them what happened in the bell chamber, but suspected they knew. She thought maybe they were jealous that the castle would share some of its magic with someone that was not a queen.

"That is why we need you to find her and bring her back," said Cinderella. Now the queens needed Zandria. "She may not be in a mood to listen to either of us," continued the queen.

Adam asked, "Do we have any idea where she might be?"

Snow White returned to her chair. Adam and Zandria joined them at the table. The wizards remained silent, apparently with nothing of value to offer. William stood next to the warrior, Aleta. Zandria thought she looked as intense as usual.

Snow White said, "Our wizards tried to track her, but if she used the Walking Portal, then we have no way of knowing where she went."

William offered, "It is my understanding that Queen Isis saw her last. The queen has since returned to the Southern Valley due to a border dispute. I recommend we seek her out, since we have no other possible leads."

"I expect Isis would have sent us word of Olena's arrival, but we have received none," said Snow White.

Zandria did not want to sit and wait at the castle. She agreed that searching in the south would be better than not searching at all. She suggested they send out the Guardian Hawks, but one of the wizards informed them that the four fastest birds were already gone on another mission.

Aleta offered, "I will go with you." Zandria liked the dark-skinned woman and gladly accepted her help. Aleta added, "It will be good to have someone with you that knows the Southern Valley." Then to William, "It will be my turn to show you my homeland."

William scolded himself, "This will be no holiday."

Zandria knew she did not have to ask Adam for his help. He already looked set to be in a saddle.

"Don't worry, Zan," he said. "We'll find her."

A short time later, the party gathered in the courtyard. Kalis and Sulis stood, waiting to leave. Fury waited with them.

"My queen has advised against it, but I'm coming with you," stated Fury.

"Thank you," said Zandria.

A fourth Friesian named Stamenor joined them. Zandria understood he was the only other surviving Friesian from Adam and William's fateful trip to the Rockhorn Mines. He also carried Aleta and Smoltz back to Castle Empyrean while William hunted the evil Lord Vanril.

Zandria, Adam, William and Aleta each mounted a Friesian. The strong horses impatiently clicked their diamond shoes on the glass courtyard while the drawbridge slowly lowered and the thorn wall parted.

In her heart, Zandria prayed for Olena's safety. Aloud, she said, "For Olena."

William added, "For the Queen of the Eastern Sky."

Fury led the horses across the fireproof bridge. In an instant, their hooves pounded the dirt road and they galloped south at their top speed.

Chapter 15

"How are you?" asked Kez.

Olena did not answer at first. She looked around the room at Kez, Karl, Sylvan in his Rockhorn body and Apis the cat. She thought about Zandria and her mother. She thought about Ovara bringing her to the Southern Valley. Then she thought about Spynum Begg attacking Queen Isis. She wanted to cry. She wanted to act like a little girl and turn her face into her pillow until all the bad thoughts left her.

She knew that could not happen though. A year ago, Olena would have been free to do whatever she wanted. As Queen of the Eastern Sky however, she knew she had a duty. She had the responsibility to face any threat to Empyrean no matter how it made her feel.

Olena knew she was not as brave as Zandria, but she wanted to be like her big sister right now.

"I'm fine," Olena lied. She did not want to give Kez and the others any need to worry about her. She did not want them to know how scared she actually was. "What happened? How did I get here?" She tried to push some of the attention off of herself.

"We found you in the catacombs," said Karl. He adjusted his glasses in a nervous gesture. "You were sleeping in one of the tunnels right near the entrance. We thought we lost you too, but we got you out right before the seals closed."

She noticed Karl said *too*. Olena hoped Isis survived the attack, but she already knew the old queen did not. She had to stifle her tears.

Kez said, "I'm sorry. The Queen of the Southern Valley has passed into the twilight."

"Spynum Begg was not only an ambassador, but also an assassin," said Karl Lumpkin.

Then one of the cat headed servants entered the room. She carried a tray with a pitcher and one glass. She sat on the edge of the bed and poured out a glass of what looked like water for Olena.

"Drink," said Apis from the foot of her bed. His tail swished gently back and forth. "It is from the River of Life and will give you strength."

Olena did feel thirsty and all of last night's screaming made her throat a little sore. She followed Apis' instructions and took the glass from the cat maiden. She gulped down the entire drink. At first, it tasted like any other water she had tasted. Then, as the cool liquid filled her belly, she felt a change. Suddenly, she had more energy and wanted to get out of bed. Her head seemed clearer and her worries felt less heavy.

The cat woman went to the door. Before she walked out, she said, "You have a visitor waiting in the throne room. Shall I tell him you will see him now?"

With renewed strength, Olena sat up. She had no idea who would be here to see her, especially at a time like this. She looked to her friends and they returned a look of confidence. Olena turned to Apis and he gave her a nod of approval.

"We will be right there," said Olena.

They gave her a few moments of privacy to change and then Rockhorn Sylvan led the way. Olena, with Kez and Apis at her side, came next and Karl followed behind them into the throne room. The identity of their visitor surprised Olena.

Horus waited for them, kneeling next to the throne.

"Your Majesty, I am glad to see you are safe," said the man with the hawk head. Olena could not believe that his beak did not affect the sound of his voice. She had met other talking animals and their beaks and muzzles usually changed the way their words came out, but his were clear and strong.

"I thought you could not come into the temple?" said Kez.

"Before now, that was true." Horus looked from Kez to Olena with his solid black eyes. "For some time, I have been working in secret for Queen Isis. It was not safe for me to come here or for us to be seen together."

Olena looked at his tan, muscular body. She could not quite get used to his bird-like head, but loved the color of his brown and white speckled feathers. They almost distracted her from the importance of their conversation.

Horus continued, "Now, with the queen gone, our enemies have revealed themselves. There is no reason for me to hide any longer."

"What are you going to do?" asked Olena.

"What can I do?" said Horus. "We have no army and the farmers who fought in your battle are still trying to recover their crops with what little water the Arcosaurans allow. Now, I fear they can take control of the entire Southern Valley."

He sounded defeated, thought Olena. Apis did not offer any suggestions either. Maybe it was the boost she felt from the Brygos water, or maybe her natural power as a queen, but Olena did not want to accept defeat.

"I know this isn't my land, but I do not accept this," she said.

Kez and Karl seemed to perk up at this. They gave her their complete attention. Olena felt slightly uncomfortable. She did not feel like a leader, but she felt they were now treating her as one.

"Well," Olena clicked her teeth, "I don't know what to do. Isis would have known. She would not allow this."

"Then you have to have some kind of plan," said Karl. "Can you call on the Friesian Army for assistance?"

"I think that would take too long" said Olena. "Maybe if I could go back to the Eternity Temple, I could see something important."

"Impossible," said Apis. "Only the Queen of the Southern Valley can enter the Eternity Temple."

"But I've already been there," said Olena.

She could tell neither Apis nor Horus believed her and she wondered if Karl did either. Olena turned to Kez for support.

"We found you, unconscious, in the catacombs. It was dark and there were a lot of long halls. Maybe you dreamt it?" said Kez.

"No. I was there. I could see the past and the future, too, I think. I saw Spynum Begg escape with some Arcosaurans and that jackal from earlier," explained Olena. "I could go back there to search for a clue. Maybe see what is going to happen?"

"Even if you could find and enter the Eternity Temple, the catacombs are sealed," said Horus. "They will not re-open until the next queen is called. The temple only reveals its secrets to the Queen of the Southern Valley. I understand they were lucky enough to find you before the stone doors closed on those tunnels."

Olena had no other suggestions. Without her own magic, she felt helpless.

"What about the Infinity Temple?" asked Karl.

"We're in the Infinity Temple, aren't we?" asked Olena.

"There is a room in the tallest tower. It is also called the Infinity Temple, that is what the entire palace is named for," said Apis. "We can try it, but I believe the power will only work for the southern queen."

On the walk to the tower, Olena told Karl and Kez what she saw in the Eternity Temple. Horus and Apis walked ahead of them. The man-bird carried a torch along the windowless stone halls.

"You saw yourself as a little girl?" asked Karl.

"I was on the beach with Zandria. It must have been a few years ago, but I don't remember it. It felt strange, not real," said Olena.

"But you saw the future as well?" asked Kez.

"It had to be Zandria's wedding day. She looked about ten years older. She was getting married to..." Olena stopped herself. She did not know if she should tell them she saw Adam. She did not want to change the future. Maybe if people knew Zandria was supposed to marry the copper-haired boy, she might stop liking him.

"Who?" pried Kez.

"I couldn't tell." Olena did not like that it was getting easier to lie to her friends. She reassured herself that it was necessary to protect them. Maybe, she thought, knowing what to say and when to say it was one of the powers of the queens. She quickly decided that lying was never a good solution. She promised she would keep this one secret, but never lie to her friends again.

"I wish I would have seen something helpful about the Arcosaurans," Olena said.

"Maybe you will see something up here," said Karl.

Horus stopped in front of what appeared to be a solid stone wall. He said, "We cannot go with you."

Olena did not know where Horus expected her to go. She could not see a door. Then she thought maybe it was a secret door like in the catacombs. She stuck out her hand in order to push on the wall. Instead, she passed right through it. Olena looked back to see the others standing in the hall as if there was no barrier between them. She waved, but obviously they could only see the imaginary stone wall and not her.

Behind her, Olena found a spiral staircase. She did not have a torch, but could see clearly by the light coming from the top of the stairs. It looked like normal sunlight.

When Olena wound her way to the top, she stood inside the tip of the pyramid that she originally saw from outside. She knew this because the room had four walls shaped like triangles that met at a point in the center. With as many stairs as they climbed, this could be the only possibility. Daylight filled the room, but Olena saw no windows. Where the windows should have been, four mirrors completely covered the four walls.

For a moment, Olena could see her own reflection. Then it vanished. She turned to the next wall and her image faded there as well. The same thing happened on the other two walls. Olena stood in a room of mirrors, but could not see herself anywhere.

"What's the point?" Olena asked aloud.

Then the four walls separated. They opened wide at the top and folded down out of sight. Olena felt the wind whip around her like on the high balconies at Castle Empyrean. Unfortunately, here she had no railings to keep her from falling. She stayed almost in the exact center, as far as she could from any of the edges.

Olena could see all of Hierakonpolis below her. She looked north and suddenly could see Lake Nata Playa as if she was standing next to it. This did not feel the same as when she looked at the Brygos with Isis back at Castle Empyrean. She could still see everything between here and the lake, but it looked impossibly small. Her vision zoomed across the land as if it were a map moving under her. Only the place she wanted to see appeared large and in focus. Everything else stayed small and out of the way.

She looked further north and saw Castle Empyrean. Now she knew it was not her power, but the power of the Infinity Temple. She watched four riders come across the drawbridge. Olena shifted her gaze and could instantly and clearly see their faces. Zandria, Adam, William and Aleta looked like they were heading out on an important task.

Then Olena wanted to see Banookanook. She did not turn her head or body. She simply thought about her old home and it filled her vision. Some of the Nookans fished as usual, but others looked hard at work on what might have been the foundation of her Palace on the Sea.

"I can see anywhere in Empyrean," Olena said. She wondered if she could even see places she had never been. She tried to remember the name that Ogustus called the western palace. "Show me Le Chateau de la Belle Eternelle."

Before her suddenly rose the most beautiful castle she had ever seen. It stood on the edge of a cliff. Flags and banners waved from countless towers and parapets. Enchanting gardens filled the courtyard and dotted the town behind the castle.

Now, Olena thought about the reason she came up here in the first place. She needed some hint for what to do about the Arcosaurans. She scanned the Unending Desert. Maybe, she thought, it was a trick of the room, but the Unending Desert seemed small for a name like that.

Olena's vision did not go past the desert. She must have reached the southern edge of Empyrean. She wanted to see more. She needed to. Then Olena's eyesight blurred. When she could focus again, she could see some grassland at the edge of the desert. Beyond that, it turned into a forest with unusual plants and trees that made her think of the jungle by Banookanook. South of the forest, the ground turned to dull, black rock. Erupting volcanoes dotted the horizon.

In the center of this depressing landscape protruded the tallest of the volcanoes. No lava came from this one, but she saw the washed out ruts left by a once great river. Olena knew they had to go there. It had to be the source of the Brygos.

The walls of the Infinity Temple started to slowly fold closed. Olena wanted to see more. She needed to see where the Arcosaurans lived.

"Wait. I'm not done," she said.

Apparently, the room was done with her. The tip of the pyramid sealed closed and Olena could see her reflection in the mirrored walls again. She went back down the stairs and found everyone still waiting for her.

"Did it work?" asked Karl.

"It worked," Olena said with a big smile.

Apis did not seem to believe her. "What did you see?"

"The far south, Arcenland," explained Olena. "The Arcosaurans are on the other side of the Unending Desert."

"We already knew that," said Horus.

"Did you know the Brygos came from a field of volcanoes?"

Apparently, neither Horus nor Apis knew the river's origins. Karl did not act like he did either. This ended their conversation for the moment.

Back in the throne room, Apis expressed his continued disbelief. "The Infinity Temple does not have the ability to see beyond the borders of Empyrean."

"But I saw it," said Olena. "I don't know how, but I think we have to go there."

Horus said, "Crossing the Unending Desert would be difficult enough, but crossing into Arcenland could be considered an act of war."

Karl sprang up from the pile of cushions where he had been reclining. "What are you? An Immortal or a politician?" he snapped at Horus.

"The Immortals don't exist anymore," said Horus.

Olena wanted to hear more about Immortals, but neither Karl nor Horus continued that conversation. They both turned their attention to her.

"You're a stranger here and can go where you please, but I cannot allow anyone from the Southern Valley to start a war," said Horus.

"I concur," said Apis.

Kez said, "In case you haven't noticed, the Arcosaurans started this war when they attacked Queen Isis."

"Spynum Begg could have been acting on his own," said Horus.

"I saw the Arcosaurans help him escape," said Olena. "You're afraid. It's okay to be afraid. I am too. If this is Emperor Li-Am's plan to help the Forgotten Evil come back, then we have to do everything we can to stop him, even if we are scared."

"I agree," said Karl. "I will go with you."

"You can count on me," said Kez.

Sylvan took a deep bow, apparently indicating he would help as well.

"Then we should make preparations to leave in the morning," said Olena.

Horus and Apis started to leave the throne room, but a cobra guard stopped them. The guard whispered to Horus and then left.

"Even if either of us wanted to go with you, it seems we have more pressing issues in Hierakonpolis," said Horus.

Karl asked, "Has the new queen already been called?"

Olena thought she could make out despair on Horus' hawk features. It seemed strange to be able to read any expression on a face like that.

Horus said, "I wish I had such news. The seals have cracked."

Karl must have understood immediately what Horus meant. He took off his broken glasses and wiped them with his sash. Then he used the sash to wipe the newly formed beads of sweat from his forehead.

What seals did Horus mean, wondered Olena. Then it occurred to her that he was talking about those horrid statues surrounding the marketplace. The seals that held back the Forgotten Evil's lieutenants.

"Does that mean they've escaped?" asked Olena. She did not want to think about such powerful enemies being free.

"We need to inspect the situation, but so far the seals are still intact," said Horus.

Karl tried to reassure Olena, "For those creatures to escape, the seals would have to be completely shattered. Only a queen or the Forgotten Evil himself would have the power to do that. Since no queen would ever open them on purpose and the old man is still in the bottomless pit, I think we are safe. Still, I would be more comfortable applying some additional binding spells."

The young alchemist left with the hawkman and the black cat. Olena, Kez and Sylvan sat alone in the dim torchlight of the throne room.

"I am sure things will be fine," said Kez.

"Even if the lieutenants escape, that doesn't mean the Forgotten Evil is back," said Olena. She tried to comfort herself by saying this.

Sylvan raised both of his weapon arms in a defensive pose. Olena understood his intentions. She thought he meant he would protect her.

While they waited for Karl to come back from the marketplace, Olena went to her room to change. She found some comfortable walking clothes, simple pants and a shirt. Then she found some boots that looked like they would keep out the sand.

Olena had a few questions on her mind. First, she wanted to know what caused the seals to crack.

Secondly, she wanted to know who the new Queen of the Southern Valley would be and when she would be called.

The last thing Olena considered was putting on the Bronze Ring again. She thought it may be better to be in disguise when she left the temple. If the Arcosaurans were still after her too, they might have their own spies, like jackals, watching the palace. She thought she might be safer in the ring. Still, she did not want to wind up trapped there either. Olena turned the ring over in her fingers while she thought about this.

"I wouldn't do that," said Kez. He must have seen her holding the ring, but he saw it too late.

Olena slipped the ring on her thumb.

Chapter 16

The second trip into the ring proved to be as jolting as the first. Olena felt like she tumbled sideways and then abruptly stopped. This upset both her stomach and her sense of balance.

Strangely, she felt slightly more comfortable with her surroundings this time. The dimly lit room seemed more familiar, more welcoming. Olena did not have to walk down the long hall. Almost as quickly as she put on the ring, she stood in the small room with the three statues.

Olena checked the mirror behind her. Kez looked upset with her. She planned to apologize later, but felt this would be the best way to leave the castle.

The statues of Ovara, Ogustus and Omarika did not move. Olena knocked on Ogustus' wide knee. She heard a faint metallic echo. Then Olena turned to try and get a response from Omarika.

"Boo," shouted Ovara.

Olena screamed in unpleasant surprise.

"I got you again," said Ovara. She wore a triumphant smile.

"That's mean," said Olena.

"Oh, am I supposed to be nice?" asked Ovara. Her expression did not look like she really cared.

Ogustus and Omarika still did not move. Olena had hoped to get some support from the rotund man.

"I thought we were supposed to help each other," said Olena.

Ovara looked indignant. "No one helped me when I got trapped in here. That guy couldn't wait to escape. He didn't care that I was only a little girl."

"What guy was that?" asked Ogustus from behind Olena.

It made Olena feel better that the big man finally joined them even though he startled her. She noticed that the silent Omarika stepped down from her pedestal as well.

"Don't worry about it," said Ovara. She looked like she got caught lying and did not want to say anything else.

Olena remembered Ogustus told her Ovara would not say who inhabited the ring before her. Now with Ovara's secretive behavior, Olena wanted to know even more. She did not think she would get any more out of Ovara now, so she did not ask.

"I suppose with your return, liddel lady, it is my turn to step outside," said Ogustus. "Thus far, you have learned our first two rules. It will be my pleasure in assisting you with the third."

Ogustus carefully made his way to the mirror. Leaning against the side, he picked up his cane. Olena had not noticed it before and guessed it only appeared when Ogustus needed it. Still, she liked the look of the carved wolf's head handle. Then Olena remembered how much Zandria disliked any type of wolf. This made her miss her sister and wish she could show Zandria this room.

Now, she watched Ogustus gingerly put his hand to the mirror as if he was checking the temperature of his bath water. Once he had his entire left arm through, Ogustus stepped through with his left leg. Then he stopped. It seemed his large belly would not fit through the opening.

"Oh," he said. "It has been a while. Odd how I can be bigger without eating anything,"

"Or maybe the mirror shrank," Ovara said facetiously.

Right before he squeezed the rest of the way out, Ogustus gave Ovara a stern look. It did not seem to bother her.

"I thought he'd never leave," said Ovara. She and Omarika went back to their platforms.

Olena turned her attention to the mirror. She concentrated as before and instantly felt like she was hovering above Ogustus' head. She could hear him introducing himself to Kez and Sylvan. From this perspective, Olena smiled at how bald Ogustus was. She discovered that the bushy hair he had on the sides of his head and his thick mustache were bright orange.

"It is my pleasure to meet you," said Ogustus.

Kez said, "That is fine, but when can we expect Olena back?"

"For now, I will be attending you," said Ogustus.

"Tell them I want to go to Arcenland in disguise," thought Olena.

Ogustus repeated Olena's wishes to her friends. "That is her desire."

When Karl returned, he must have stopped to change his clothes back into his comfortable western attire. His vest matched this outfit much better than last night's dinner clothes. He also tied a jacket around his waist.

"What's that for?" asked Kez.

"Desert nights can get cold," explained Karl. Then, almost like an afterthought, he referred to Ogustus. "Is this the new queen?"

"Indeed," laughed Ogustus. "You have a wonderful sense of humor, my young alchemist."

Karl looked impressed. He said, "You've heard of the great Karl Lumpkin?"

"Sadly no, but I've met more than a few alchemists during my time in the western courts," said Ogustus.

"Knowing you're from the west, with the look of you and that wonderful cane, I would say you served under the second Queen of the Western Sun," said Karl. It sounded like a guess to Olena, but he looked certain. "I have heard of you."

"Say no more," Ogustus said with a wink.

However, Olena did want to know more. Ogustus' behavior seemed suspicious toward Karl and she could feel in his heart that he was hiding something. Karl knowing his identity apparently made Ogustus nervous for some reason.

Then she felt a tapping on her shoulder. Through her connection, Olena could not see anyone tapping Ogustus' shoulder. It took her a moment to realize the sensation was actually happening to her in the bronze room. Olena opened her eyes to find Ovara picking at her.

"You wanna know a secret?" asked Ovara.

Being pulled away from Ogustus annoyed Olena. She believed she needed to pay attention to the big man, especially with him acting so mysterious.

"It's about Ogustus," continued Ovara.

This did catch Olena's attention. Maybe Ovara knew what Ogustus was hiding about his time at Le Chateau de la Belle Eternelle.

Ovara led Olena to Ogustus' pedestal. The stubborn girl climbed up into the big chair. She looked small on the wide seat. Ovara then patted the hard metal cushion next to her, presumably inviting Olena to join her. Olena accepted the invitation and quickly learned that a bronze cushion was not nearly as soft as a real cushion.

"What do you know about Ogustus?" asked Olena.

"I know he's better at keeping secrets than I am."

Olena took this chance to ask, "Tell me who was in the ring before you?"

"Except that secret. That one's mine. But we've been in here a long time and the big guy's told me plenty of other stories," said Ovara.

"Then tell me about Ogustus," said Olena. She decided not to press Ovara. If they became better friends, Olena felt Ovara would eventually share more about her past.

She watched Ovara's metal face crease with a slight smile. Then the girl that reminded her of a mean version of Zandria began her story.

"So far, our friend has only said he served in the western court. He was telling the truth. He did serve there for a short time."

"That guy Karl recognized him because of his famous cane. If you saw that cane, it meant you'd been had." This seemed to make Ovara smile, but she quickly hid it.

"Ogustus is very smart. He was actually an advisor to the second Queen of the Western Sun. He won many debates and settled many arguments. He also loved puzzles. There was not one riddle or trick box he couldn't solve. It got to be a challenge to anyone that came to the Chateau. No one could beat Ogustus."

"He started going to secret meetings in backrooms and cellars searching for more difficult and dangerous challenges. He even started to wager money on his ability," Ovara continued.

"When he finally lost, he lost everything. The con-artist that beat him tricked Ogustus into betting all of his money. The queen learned of

Ogustus gambling and barred him from the castle."

"Ogustus swore revenge on the man who cheated him. Now Ogustus is vague on the next part, but this part of the story ends with the con-artist never being seen again. I guess there are many isolated cliffs in the west and things probably fall off of them all the time."

"With no money and no job, Ogustus had to find a new way to survive. Like the man who ruined his life, Ogustus turned to ruining others. He used his talent in order to trick and cheat others out of their possessions. Wherever he went, no one remembered his face, but they all remembered his cane."

"He insists the cane was a gift from some men that could turn into wolves," finished Ovara.

"Werewolves," interrupted Olena, "but they're bad."

Ovara continued, "Supposedly not this family. Since the First War for Empyrean, they have lived hidden in the western mountains. That's what Ogustus says anyway."

The story made Olena sad. Of the three Inhabitants, she actually liked Ogustus the best. She favored him over Omarika only because she did not talk and that made her nervous. This news made her doubt Ogustus though. If he really was a con-artist, Olena knew she could not trust him.

Without another word, Ovara went back to her own spot and froze. Olena had nothing else to do, except reconnect with Ogustus.

As soon as she concentrated, Olena shivered, Ogustus and her friends were camping in the middle of the Unending Desert. They must have left Hierakonpolis while she listened to Ovara's story. Now, night had fallen and cold and darkness surrounded them.

"Ah," said Ogustus. He must have felt her presence. Then he silently thought, "I'm sorry you had to learn it from her. She sometimes takes pleasure in making others look less than they are."

Olena understood he could read her heart and thoughts as easily as she could read his. He could tell she knew the truth about him.

Ogustus continued thinking, "I know you doan trust me, but that was a long time ago. Remember, before that, I was a gut man."

"But are you good now?" came Olena's reply. She still wanted to trust him.

"That is for you to decide," answered Ogustus.

In the morning, Olena got a good look at the Unending Desert. She could only see sand in every direction. They had travelled far enough away from the city not to see even the tallest pyramids or obelisks. Still, they had not gone far enough to see the strange forest at the edge of Arcenland that she saw in her vision, or whatever it was. This desert seemed much smaller from the top of the Infinity Temple.

Even though Karl seemed to know the truth about Ogustus, he did not treat him any different as the day progressed. In fact, Olena though Karl responded to Ogustus as if he was speaking directly to her.

They made their way slowly as the sun beat down on them. Ogustus had the most difficult time as his cane kept sinking into the sand with each swagger of his wide body. By late afternoon, Olena did not think the big man could move any longer.

Before he asked for a rest, Olena noticed something on the horizon. It looked like an old man with a long beard coming toward them. Olena guided Ogustus' view in that direction. Thankful for the stop, he pointed out the visitor to Kez and Karl. The party waited for the stranger to come to them as he moved much quicker than they could.

As the bearded man came closer, Olena could see his true shape. While he did have the head of a man and a long white beard, he did not have a man's body. Instead, he walked on the four legs of a lion. This particular lion easily stood as tall as Fury, if not taller.

His white hair and beard made him look quite old. However, with the pleats and braids in all of his hair, he looked well groomed. Even with a lion's body, Olena would not have been scared except for the other features.

This man had huge bird wings on his back. Olena knew they were not hawk wings and Ogustus' western knowledge told her they were eagle wings. She recognized the most frightening feature without any help. A long scorpion's tail curled up from his backside.

The whole time they waited, this unusual man did not run or change his pace. He came directly toward them as if he had been expecting them. Finally, he stood close enough to strike them with his pointed tail if he chose to do that. Only Sylvan did not look small next to this man-beast.

He spoke with a melodious horn-like voice, "Greetings. I am Phix. I understand you wish to cross my desert."

No one prepared Olena for this. They only spoke briefly with Horus and Apis about crossing the Unending Desert. From Kez and Karl's expressions, she guessed no one gave them any warnings about needing permission either.

Karl said, "My apologies. I have only lived in the south for a few years. I did not realize anyone had ownership of this land."

Phix swished his terrifying tail. He said, "I have been the guardian of the Unending Desert since time began. Immortals beg for my blessings."

"Good thing none of us are Immortals," said Karl. "So we'll be going then?"

"This is my land and I will decide who sets foot on it," said Phix. He curled his tail as if preparing to strike.

"Doan be too hasty," said Ogustus. Olena could feel his uncertainty. He thought Phix meant to attack them.

"Right. You know we are not the only ones crossing your desert," said Kez.

"The Arcosaurans are troublesome," said Phix.

"They intend to take this land all the way to Hierakonpolis as their own," added Kez.

Phix sat down on the warm, golden sand with his front paws out in front of him. He let his tail relax and stretched his wings for a moment.

"If that is their purpose, then what is yours?" asked Phix.

Kez continued to speak for the group, "We plan to stop their invasion."

"That seems unlikely, but anyone that can answer my riddle shall be granted safe passage from me," said Phix.

"And if we cannot?" asked Karl.

Before Olena realized what happened, Phix lashed out with his deadly tail. The creature speared a piece of fruit with its pointed tip right out of Karl's satchel. Phix had it in his mouth and completely chewed in an instant.

Olena could feel Ogustus getting excited. She knew he could solve any riddle. He bubbled with confidence and took delight in the opportunity. Olena hesitated. She did not know if she should trust her and her friends' lives to this con-artist.

Before she could make a decision, Ogustus said, "Ask me your riddle, old one."

The creature tilted his human head to the side. He seemed to be estimating Ogustus. Then he closed his eyes as if trying to remember something important. When Phix opened his eyes, he said, "Through mists of time or sand through a glass, there has been only one that would surpass. In the past growing older, in confidence growing bolder. Always four, but once only one. What am I?"

Olena felt a flash like Ogustus immediately knew the answer, but he did not say it. He stopped to ponder the question. Olena thought about it as well. It seemed to her that the answer had to be about the Unending Desert, or maybe the ancient trees of the Northern Wood. Then she wondered how something could grow older in the past. She knew some trees in Great Wood Forest were over one thousand years old, but they only got older as time moved forward. She thought another possibility might have to do with the Euphoric Mountains. Olena knew there were mists at the top of the mountains. She decided this could not be right either because there were far more than four peaks.

Then Ogustus thought to her, "Liddel lady, if you do not trust me, at least trust yourself. Listen to your heart. Does it tell you I know the answer? Riddles are my specialty and I would not seal your fate with one as simple as this."

Olena did feel it in her heart that Ogustus believed he knew the answer. Maybe she did not trust him, but she had to trust herself and her own intuition. She agreed to let him answer for them all.

"Oh venerable Phix," began Ogustus, "I think you try to mislead us with talk of your sandy domain. It is true that the passage of time is something with which we all struggle. Perhaps some do not age too fast? You know as well as I that none age in reverse, which leaves me with one possibility. Your riddle is about a person falling backwards through time. Only then, could that person grow older in the past." Ogustus held up his wolf-headed cane, "Also true that there are usually four. However, this time only one did surpass many great challenges."

Ogustus still did not answer, but Olena thought she could guess from his words. She believed the riddle could only be about the four queens of Empyrean. In her head, Ogustus said, "Not four queens."

Aloud, Ogustus continued, "But only one. What am I you ask? I am the Passing Queen."

"Ugh," Olena said to herself. "Does everyone know about the Passing Queen except me?"

Phix silently nodded that Ogustus had given the correct answer. Passage to his land had been granted.

Chapter 17

𓅂 ▭ ⸗ 𓂋 ● 𓊪 𓅂 ● ⸗

Phix escorted them the rest of the way across the Unending Desert. Olena did not understand the name of this desert. Instead of unending, it seemed rather small. She wanted to ask Phix, but he scared her a little. However, once Ogustus solved the riddle, Olena did not think Phix seemed that menacing. He actually seemed rather friendly.

"It should not take us long to cross," explained the creature. "The desert is not very big."

"Then why do they call it Unending?" asked Kez for Olena.

"That is the secret," answered Phix. "As one of the borders of Empyrean, you should be able to guess it is protected by Deep Magic. For many, the desert continues to expand and they never reach their destination. Only those that have my blessing may cross quickly and safely."

Karl asked, "What about Spynum Begg and the Arcosaurans?"

"That is a riddle I do not have the answer to. Some magic aides them and hides them from my sight," said Phix.

They walked on in silence for a while, always at a pace slow enough for Ogustus. Olena wished she could do something for him. He seemed to have a difficult time moving his large body. She could feel his frustration because his mind worked incredibly fast. His rotund body had no chance of keeping up with it.

Before long, yellowish-green grass poked up out of the sand. Soon, the grass completely replaced the sand. Olena's friends stood in a wide field and she could see tall trees in the distance.

"This is Arcenland," said Phix. "I will leave you now. It appears I must keep a sharper eye on my desert."

Olena urged Ogustus to say, "Thank you."

Phix, already with his back to them, did not turn around when he replied, "Do not thank me. I would have eaten you as easily as not."

Then the man with the lion's body padded off across the Unending Desert and out of sight.

"Can't trust anybody," said Karl, jokingly.

Olena thought about this seriously for a moment though. She believed good people lived throughout Empyrean. She believed she could trust anybody. She wanted to trust everybody. Maybe because she was so young, Olena found it easy to trust without questioning.

She thought about Ogustus, trying to hide her feelings from him. Even though he had done bad things, he seemed kind. Besides, he had helped so far. Then Olena realized it was not the man she trusted, but herself. She trusted her own heart and instincts about him. Then he took that trust and solved the riddle.

"That's it," said Ogustus.

He appeared next to Olena in the bronze room. A big smile spread across his face. With the connection broken, Olena could not read his thoughts to tell what made him so happy.

Ogustus continued, "Liddel lady, see how quickly you learn? So soon you have discovered the third rule. Trust yourself."

"Trust myself," Olena repeated, almost not sure what rule she learned.

The big man made his way to his seat. He looked relieved to be back in the ring and not in the blazing sun. Olena did not think Ovara felt the same when she came back.

"Yes, trust yourself. Your heart does not lie to you. It knows the difference between right and wrong. Some call this a conscience, others inspiration. In either case, let it guide you."

"Trust myself, have faith and listen with my heart," said Olena, repeating the rules she had learned so far. She wanted to ask about the fourth rule.

Before she could ask, the mirror pulled her backwards. When she appeared in Arcenland, Olena lost her balance and toppled onto her bottom.

Olena thought she heard the faintest whisper from Ogustus. It sounded like he was talking to Ovara or Omarika and not to her, then the sound faded to nothing.

He said, "Doan worry, she'll be back. The temptation is too great."

What did he mean by this, wondered Olena. Clearly, he meant she would be back in the ring again. But why would they worry, she thought. Did they think she would abandon them or were they hiding some other type of secret? She did not like the idea of being trapped in the ring and thought maybe she could try not to use it again. Still, something made her want to put it on her thumb. Ogustus called it a temptation.

For now, Olena resisted. She wanted to see Arcenland. Only a few days ago, Olena felt trapped in her bedroom. She not only went to the southern Valley, but now set foot in a foreign land. A land she did not know even existed a few days ago.

Arcenland seemed familiar, but also very different. Large rocks, or maybe small boulders, dotted the wide field. The grass did not grow as high as it did on the central plains around Castle Empyrean, but it looked softer. Olena ran her hands through it as she sat there and found the grass to be quite soft. She thought with a nice breeze, she could easily take a nap in this peaceful field.

Kez interrupted her daydream. He said, "I'm glad to have you back."

Olena almost forgot that wearing the ring separated her from her friends. While she could see and hear them, they could not do likewise. It must be weird watching her disappear and reappear, she thought.

"It's good to be back," she said.

"Back? From where exactly?" asked Karl.

She did not know how to explain it, but Olena tried.

"It's a room. I don't know where it's at. Maybe inside the ring," she said. Olena held up her hand, palm down to show off the ring.

"Could be," said Karl. He looked at the ring closely, gently holding her hand steady. "Does it feel cramped?"

A deep, echoing sound interrupted their conversation. Olena thought it was some kind of animal cry, but it sounded too loud. It would have to be a huge animal to make a sound like that, thought Olena. She found comfort in that it also sounded quite far from them.

"I think that noise came from beyond those trees," Kez said, pointing at the tree line a short walk in the distance.

"I'm afraid that's where we're going," said Olena. Deep down, she did feel some fear. She knew at least some of the Arcosaurans followed the Forgotten Evil. To make things worse, they did not look human. From the glimpse she had in the Eternity Temple, they looked like monsters.

Kez scurried up Sylvan's leg and took a safe spot on his stone shoulder. Karl offered Olena his hand. For a brief moment, Olena wondered what it would be like to have a big brother. She liked the idea of having someone who had to protect her. Plus, she could also tell him to fix his messy hair.

Olena took Karl's hand and he pulled her up from the ground where she had been since coming out of the ring. Then the four of them headed into the forest.

Many of the plants reminded Olena of the jungle near Banookanook. They grew low to the ground with wide, lush leaves. The trees stood far apart. When two did grow close together, one of them was usually smashed. Olena tried to imagine something so big that it had to knock trees over when it walked. If the trees grew too close, they must block the pathways for some pretty enormous creatures, she guessed. Then she realized she did not want to imagine something like that.

As they went further into the woods, Olena began hearing all sorts of strange noises. She guessed many of them to be birds, high above their heads. Still, some of the hoots and roars sounded bigger, like the first noise they heard. Far off to their left, she heard a tree crash. It made Olena very thankful to not be going in that direction.

The trees looked bigger as they progressed. Olena looked behind them and saw the rise. The trees in this part of the forest definitely grew taller than those closer to the desert. They also stood much further apart than their smaller neighbors.

These trees seemed to be extremely old. Many of them grew so tall that their tops were out of sight. The space between them increased as well. It felt like maybe she and her friends shrank to the size of bugs and did not realize it.

Eventually, they came to a clearing. Olena felt better being able to see the sun. In the forest, the leaves mostly blocked it way up high, but it was not unpleasant darkness like in the Dead Forest. Now, it felt like she could almost touch the sun. It seemed bigger than she remembered. However, it did not feel hotter than back in the desert. Maybe they were up higher now, she guessed.

Here, they found themselves between two great walls. Behind, Olena looked at the empty forest. In front of her, stood rows of hills that led to an immense cliff.

At least, it looked like a cliff to Olena. However, when she looked at an angle to her right, she could see an opening in the cliff face that started from the ground up. The mountainside did not look very wide. It looked more like a cliff on both sides. It could have been a naturally occurring wall, she suspected. This wall got narrower as it went higher. She did not think there would even be enough room for her and Karl to stand side-by-side at the top. If they could make the steep climb to the top, far above them, that is.

Then Olena looked to her left. Threading between the low hills and squatty palm trees came the most peculiar parade Olena had ever seen.

The creatures came from behind the cliff wall into the wide space at the edge of the forest. None of them appeared to be the leader, but they all seemed to be going to the same place.

"These must be Arcosaurans," said Olena. The enormous, unusual creatures amazed her. She wanted to get closer.

Then Karl grabbed her and pulled her behind a tree. An instant later, a huge foot came down where Olena had been standing. The creature would have squashed her completely if Karl had not pulled her clear.

Olena followed the leg upward with her eyes. Each of the animals four legs looked like tree stumps attached to an unbelievably wide body. She almost could not tell the difference between the front and back of the animal because it had an equally long neck and tail. However, it raised its tiny head on the front end, while its tail waved through the air far behind it. It felt like the beast shook the entire land with each step, yet she did not notice it until it was almost literally on top of her.

"Sauropod," said Karl.

The beast took another step that ended with a boom on the ground.

"What?" asked Olena, not wanting to look away from the parade.

"That's a Sauropod. Even though they were supposed to be extinct, I once took the opportunity to study the Arcosaurans," explained Karl.

Olena watched the Sauropod continue, apparently unaware of them. This one looked nothing like her first sighting of Spynum Begg's conspirators. It had gray skin that looked as thick as a hippopotamus or crocodile. And, of course, it was much bigger.

Then four smaller Arcosaurans ran past, winding between the Sauropod's legs. They had wide beaks for mouths, like ducks, and ran mostly on their hind legs. Occasionally, they would drop down and use their shorter front legs too.

"What are those?" asked Olena. She almost laughed out loud at their antics. Besides, being fast, the four small Arcosaurans also appeared very playful. They nipped at each other's tails and tried to tackle each other.

Karl adjusted his glasses. Peering through the cracked lens like it did not bother him, he said, "Hadrodons."

Sauropods and Hadrodons, Olena repeated to herself. The names sounded so exotic to her. For a moment, she thought Karl might be making them up from his own imagination.

"Look out, here comes a Centuru," said Karl.

Something, looking more like an oversized bug than the other Arcosaurans, rushed by them. However, it resembled no bug in the east that Olena had ever seen. The Centuru looked half as tall as a Friesian and maybe three times longer. Ten round segments made up its body and each segment had ten legs, five to a side.

"That's one hundred legs," said Kez, as the Centuru chugged out of sight.

So many different Arcosaurans of all sizes and shapes ranging from the Hadrodons to the Sauropods ambled along toward the same destination. Karl Lumpkin, as smart as he appeared to be, could not name them all. Even the ones he did name, Olena could not remember because they were so confusing.

"Time to find out where they're going, I expect," said Karl.

"You want to follow them?" said Kez. "What if they want to hurt us?"

Karl looked at the quzzak and then to Olena. She did not know quite how to read the expression on his face. She thought he looked sometimes like he already knew what would happen. She did not think he had ever been to the Eternity Temple, but he talked like the future already happened for him. Maybe he had a good reason for going after them, she wondered.

In Olena's heart, she felt following these particular Arcosaurans would be the right thing to do.

Olena said, "Ka. Let's go."

They followed the parade along the tree line well into the night. All the while, more Arcosaurans came from out of the forest and from behind the cliff wall. By the time they reached their destination, Olena guessed there were over three hundred Arcosaurans.

It felt liked they had continued walking south the whole time. The path eventually widened until Olena could see neither the forest nor the wall. In the darkness though, she realized they might not have been that far away.

Before they stopped, Olena heard Karl talking to Kez. He said, "Stop your worrying. If they wanted to eat us, they would have done it by now." The talk of being eaten made Olena's stomach growl. She hoped they would have a chance to look for their own food soon.

In the center of this new clearing, Olena noticed a faint yellow glow. The slight strobe of it growing brighter and then dimmer pulled her to it. Olena went toward the light without saying anything to Kez, Karl or Sylvan. The recent thoughts of hunger slipped from her mind as curiosity overpowered her.

Olena had to navigate through the many Arcosaurans now sitting or lying across the field surrounding the light. She did not seem to bother any of the creatures who either ate or slept. When she came close, Olena could make out a ring of stones. Each stone looked slightly taller than Sylvan's Rockhorn body and they were planted so close that she could see only one entrance.

Olena stopped, not sure whether to enter the circle or not. Something made her think she needed to do it. But whoever or whatever waited inside would know her true identity. Then Olena thought about putting on the Bronze Ring. She remembered Ogustus' words about temptation and resisted the urge. At this point, it was probably already too late anyway, she imagined.

She looked back, hoping to see Kez coming to stop her. She wanted to go in, but it scared her and she would gladly let Kez talk her out of it. Olena guessed she left her friends while they were looking for food. Either they found it or were still looking. In any event, they must not have noticed her missing yet. Without anyone to convince her otherwise, Olena decided to step into the stone circle.

A somber voice said, "We've been expecting you."

Chapter 18

Inside the circle, Olena found the most unusual Arcosaurans she had seen so far. The stones sticking out of the ground stood tall enough and close enough to make this area completely private. They were also hidden from her view until she was inside.

With so many Arcosaurans in the circle, Olena should have felt crowded. However, the sphere of yellow light in the center somehow made it seem like they had plenty of space. Wisps of light slipped off the main ball as if a breeze blew through their meeting area. Olena could not feel a breeze, but she felt warmth whenever a tail of the yellow light came close to her. She also thought she could see countless tiny stars suspended in the light.

Before she could turn her attention away from the light and back to the Arcosaurans, Karl stepped up behind her.

"Weren't starting without me, were you?" he asked. He grinned, and then adjusted his glasses. "Olena, have you met everyone here?"

Olena, of course, had not. She liked Karl and he seemed to know at least a little about almost everything. Still, she wondered if she was not supposed to be in this meeting alone.

Karl continued, "This may be conjecture on my part, but I'll handle the introductions. If my research is accurate, I believe I know everybody here."

He walked around the circle confidently, starting at Olena's left side. Olena looked at each Arcosauran as he said their names.

The first pair appeared to be only short mounds of flesh. They had no arms or legs, only body, but thankfully they did not resemble the statues back at the Hierakonpolis market. Orange skin covered their bodies and bumps as big as Olena's fists covered their skin. She could not see a face or mouth anywhere on these two creatures.

"Please meet the Sicoglitrents," said Karl.

Suddenly, almost every knobby stalk on their bodies opened to reveal eyes. One hundred pairs of eyes all staring at her and blinking randomly made Olena feel a little uncomfortable. The Sicoglitrents did not say anything in return or even reveal a mouth with which to smile politely.

Karl moved to the next group of what appeared to be three young ladies. They wore small two-piece outfits, like the warrior woman, Aleta. They reminded Olena of the handmaids back at the Infinity Temple. They had very physically fit bodies, but no tails. Also, instead of cat heads, they had very different heads. Each woman had three horns, one on each side of the forehead. The third horn poked out on a short snout where the nose should have been. In place of hair, a frill rose up on the back of each of the women's heads. It looked to Olena like their skulls actually grew out into a fan shape protecting the back of their head and neck. Each had very decorative and different colorful designs painted on their frills, cheeks, necks and shoulders. The one in front that looked like their leader also had artwork on her arms, legs and stomach.

"These lovely young ladies are the Trisariens," continued Karl.

He moved quickly around to the other side of the group. Karl seemed to be enjoying himself as he showed off his knowledge. At first, Olena did not see any Arcosaurans on this side, and then Karl became blurry. Olena quickly realized it was not her eyesight. Karl stood behind some creatures that were almost completely invisible. From the dim light of the yellow orb, Olena could not see a definite shape or how many individuals looked back at her. She thought there might be more than one, maybe as many as five. They seemed to shimmer and reflect the sparkling light. Karl waved at her from behind them and this made Olena giggle.

"I doubted we would see any Thyresoterns. I guess, technically, we still haven't, but they're in this general area," said Karl, waving a hand in front of him.

Then the somber voice from before spoke, "It is likely you will never have the opportunity again. Those of us gathered here are the last of our kind."

At the far end of the group, Olena could see the Arcosauran who that voice belonged to. He looked very much like a human-sized Sauropod, except that he stood on two legs, not four. He had a long tail and an equally long neck. Instead of waving in the air, his tail dragged on the ground. His neck also had a deep curve where his head hung low out in front of him. Olena guessed this was because of his age. He seemed to be extremely old, so much that he could barely hold up his small head.

One other thing made him appear different from the larger Sauropods, he wore clothes. This Arcosauran wore exquisite robes. Olena thought they looked nicer than most of the robes in her closet at Castle Empyrean. He must be some kind of great leader, she thought.

"I am the Parasauratitan." His voice came out deep and soothing. Olena could hear a distant echo in the sound. She also thought she could feel a vibration when he spoke, but that had to be her imagination.

"The more Immortals I meet," said Karl, "the less I think they have all vanished."

Olena became excited. She said, "You're an Immortal?"

The Parasauratitan nodded. At least, she thought the slight dip of his head looked like a nod.

"We did not meet here to discuss me," said the Parasauratitan. He slowly looked around the group and the other Arcosaurans nodded in a gesture of agreement.

"Then why did you come together?" asked Karl.

"You may have heard of Li-Am," started the Parasauratitan. "He is a Carcharodan, the most vicious of Arcosaurans. Li-Am declared himself Emperor almost five hundred years ago. He has since hunted and destroyed anyone that refuses to obey him."

"So, all of the Carcharodans follow him, of course?" said Karl. "What about the Baharians?"

The Parasauratitan continued, "The Baharians have aligned with Li-Am. They have enslaved the Majungahans as well. I am impressed that you know so much of Arcenland for a human."

"You'd be surprised by what I know," said Karl. Then he winked at Olena.

This made her think briefly about her earlier suspicions and that ominous note scrawled onto the wall of his house. She noticed Karl said and did many unusual things. He seemed to know about both the past and future. He did not come right out and say it though. He also talked about things that he could not possibly know like other people's secrets. Olena knew there was more to Karl, but now was not the time to worry about it.

"You did not mention the Spinolock," said Karl.

Olena did not like the sound of that one, but the Parasauratitan's response made her feel better.

"They are all extinct," he said.

"Before we came here, I had a vision at the Eternity Temple," said Olena. "A man named Spynum Begg escaped into the Unending Desert with the help of some green-skinned Arcosaurans, all riding on two-legged creatures."

"In part, that is why we are here. Spynum Begg is in league with Li-Am. Those that helped him escape were Baharians and bare some resemblance to humans. They rode on Majungahans. Those beasts were mindless slaves at first, but have come to savor the taste of flesh and violence. Now they eagerly serve their masters," said the Parasauratitan.

Karl asked, "In part? You said Begg is part of the reason for this meeting, what is the other part?"

The Parasauratitan raised his arm and pointed at Olena with one of his three long, boney fingers. He said, "You."

Olena's heart raced. With each new development, she wished more to be back, safe at Castle Empyrean. She thought she wanted to travel and have adventures like Zandria. She realized now that Zandria must leave all the scary parts out of her exciting stories. Olena did not want to be the center of attention either. She did not want to be the reason for anything.

"Why me?" she asked. "I'm only a little kid."

"True, but you are also a queen of Empyrean," said the Parasauratitan.

"Queen of the Eastern Sky to be exact," said Karl.

Olena could not believe Karl told them. She did not think these Arcosaurans were dangerous, but they were involved in something that was. Before they left Hierakonpolis, they agreed to keep her identity a secret and now Karl tells the first strangers they meet. At this point, she could only trust that he knew what he was doing.

The Parasauratitan looked directly at her with his round, unblinking, black eyes. "Empyrean is only a small part of our world, but it is home of the Deep Magic. As my power fades, I ask for the help of a queen's magic."

"But," started Olena. She wanted to say her magic did not work, however, Karl interrupted her.

"We will do what we can. Spynum Begg and Emperor Li-Am assassinated the Queen of the Southern Valley. This queen here has sworn to stop the servants of the Forgotten Evil. Lead us straight to Li-Am's door."

Olena already felt helpless without her powers. Now Karl gave her the added pressure of helping the Arcosaurans. She had no real idea what she intended to do when she left the Infinity Temple. She felt angry and frightened with what happed to Isis. What was a little girl supposed to do to stop an army of monsters, she asked herself.

Before Olena could think of anything to say, Sylvan entered the circle with Kez on his shoulder.

Kez said, "It is our duty to protect the Queen of the Eastern Sky. I apologize for eavesdropping, but we cannot allow her to go any further without our consent."

In his Rockhorn body, Sylvan stood taller than any of the Arcosaurans present. This seemed to catch the attention of the Parasauratitan.

He said to Olena, "Are you sure you can trust these two? It seems that the little one pays tribute to the Carcharodans."

"What do you mean?" asked Olena.

Karl studied Sylvan. He said, "I can't believe I didn't see it before."

The Parasauratitan said, "This stone creature is a replica of a Carcharodan warrior. Although, the size may be a little short."

A Rockhorn looked like a Carcharodan, the comparison shocked Olena. She did not want to think that the meanest of Arcosaurans could have weapons like a Rockhorn and maybe even be bigger. How could Vanril's dwarves known to carve the Rockhorns like this, she wondered. The only explanation seemed to be that these followers of the Forgotten Evil had met sometime in the past several hundred years. Olena knew it took Vanril a hundred years to create his army, but he would have had to get the idea and design sometime before that. He must have come south from fleeing the Northern Wood after his original revolt two hundred years ago. It was bad luck for all of the east that he chose there to dig his mine and ruin the Royal Forest.

In regards to Kez and Sylvan, Olena explained, "These are my friends."

"It's true," added Karl. "The stone giant is a prize captured from a recent battle. The creators must have somehow been inspired by Emperor Li-Am and his kind. It's perfectly harmless now. I made the modifications myself."

"Even so, it tells me Li-Am's reach has grown long," said the Parasauratitan. "It is not enough for him to control the river these past three hundred years. Now he plans to take over the Southern Valley and clearly has alliances across Empyrean."

Olena knew she had to stop this evil emperor. Without her Walking Portal, she could not go back for help in time. Maybe she did not have the power, but no one else in the south did either apparently. Even if she did not want to do it, she had an obligation.

"Tell me what to do," she said.

"It's too dangerous," said Kez. He jumped down at her feet. Olena knelt to his height.

"Why did you let me come this far then?" Olena asked.

"It was not what I intended," started Kez. "I mean, first with Ovara, then Queen Isis, everything happened so fast."

"It's okay," Olena said.

"But I need to keep you safe," said Kez. "You're my friend, but you're almost like my daughter too. I've been with you since the day you were born."

This brought a tear to Olena's eye. She knew Kez had his own quzzak children, but they were grown adults with their own children as far back as she could remember. She never thought about it like that, but he had always been there. She could always confide in him and ask for advice. He could easily have stayed in the jungle when the werewolves chased them from their home. However, he came with her and her sister. Kez was her family and she regretted not realizing it before now. Having him here and protecting her gave Olena renewed confidence.

She stood up and said to the Parasauratitan, "No one that serves the Forgotten Evil or threatens Empyrean shall thrive under my rule. I may be a child and my magic may not work great, but I am going to stop Li-Am. He will pay for what he has done to Isis."

The Parasauratitan seemed impressed. He looked around the circle to the Sicoglitrents, Trisariens and Thyresoterns in silent agreement.

He said, "It is an honor to have such an excellent queen standing before me. I do wish I could pledge more resources to our cause. Sadly, all I can promise is safe passage to the volcanic fields."

"You're not coming with us?" said Kez. "You expect her to fight your battle for you?"

"We are no army," said the Parasauratitan.

"What about the Sauropods?" Kez asked.

"What are left of our friends are the brainless creatures. They gather when we do on their instinct alone. They have no mind for good or evil. Li-Am has hunted the truly powerful Arcosaurans that opposed him. As I said before, we are the very last of our kind."

Kez looked angry. Olena tried to pick him up, but he pulled away from her. She did not worry that the Parasauratitan or his friends were not going to help. She did not want this to turn into another battle. From the sound of it, it would be a battle they could not win. As long as she had Kez and Sylvan, Olena believed she would be fine. Also, she thought she could trust Karl Lumpkin, plus she still had the Bronze Ring.

"I can offer you rest and protection for tonight," said the Parasauratitan. "We will not be here when you awake in the morning. It is not safe for us to stay in one place for too long."

One of the Trisarien women led Olena and her friends from the circle. They found a comfortable spot alongside a massive, sleeping Sauropod where they spent the night. Its deep, rhythmic snoring almost reminded her of the gentle roll of the waves on the beach.

While she slept, Olena dreamt of being back in the stone circle with the Parasauratitan. This time, they were alone.

He said, "The queens have been touched with the lifeline of the Immortals, but you also share the Deep Magic that we do not have. I cannot be more help than this, but I freely give you the last of my power."

The glowing yellow sphere at the center of the circle began to unravel. It spread out in star filled tendrils, winding their way toward her. Soon, Olena felt completely wrapped in the warm caresses of light. She felt the sparkling energy soak into her body.

When the light faded, Olena could no longer see the Parasauratitan. Her dream ended and she slept peacefully the rest of the night.

Chapter 19

The next morning, Olena woke to much fewer Arcosaurans than she saw the night before. The larger ones must have scattered when the others left the council.

Kez and Karl were already awake and talking quietly a short distance away. They must not have wanted to wake her too early. Before Olena moved to see what Kez and Karl were talking about, she tried to remember her dream. She thought she remembered the Parasauratitan giving his powers to her. Even though she slept only on the ground, she felt well rested and refreshed. She guessed this to be one of the benefits from the new power.

Is that all the Parasauratitan offered though, to feel energized? Olena wondered if there was something more to the dream or if it happened at all.

Olena wanted to know if the old Arcosauran somehow helped her magic. She decided to try a simple technique that Isis taught her. She concentrated on Kez and thought about food. After a moment, the quzzak stopped talking to Karl in mid-sentence. He walked the short distance back to her, past the stone circle.

When he came close enough, Kez asked, "I was wondering if you would like some breakfast?"

"That's so nice," said Olena. "What made you think of that?" She hoped it was her powers.

"Not sure, but it seemed like a good idea."

This delighted Olena. She believed she put the thought in his head. Queen Isis told her the queens could do this with very important matters or in times of need. She felt a little guilty using her ability for something so simple, but she wanted to see if it would work. Normally, she told herself, she would not use her power to take advantage of others. Kez quickly scampered off to find her some breakfast.

With renewed confidence, Olena decided to try the Walking Portal. She hoped she could do it without help from the ring Inhabitants. If she could create a Walking Portal, then she would take them straight to Emperor Li-Am.

But then what, she asked herself.

No one had talked about what they were going to do or say when they got there. Olena wondered if they tried to talk to him, would he even listen. She guessed not because he served the Forgotten Evil. She knew they had no chance of fighting either. Maybe Karl or Kez had come up with a plan, she hoped.

Olena still wanted to try her Walking Portal though. If she could at least form one, that would be something. She told herself she would not go through the portal without talking to the others first.

She stuck out her arms and touched her thumbs in the familiar way. She tried to imagine where they might find Li-Am. She did not know if the Carcharodans lived in a castle or a cave. Olena decided if she concentrated on the Emperor and the huge volcano, the Walking Portal would do the rest. Then she turned her hands inward so her fingertips could complete the triangle.

Nothing happened.

This saddened Olena and relieved her at the same time. She wanted desperately for all of her magic to work. She thought the extra power from the Parasauratitan would help. Maybe it was only a dream? Still, if the portal did form, they would only be a few steps from the Emperor. She did not think she was ready for that.

Luckily, no one saw her trying to do the Walking Portal. She could imagine Kez being quite upset by it. He had gone to gather some fruit and only now came back to her. They ate together, watching the huge Sauropods breakfasting on the leafy tops of some nearby trees. She did not tell him about the dream.

Almost all of the friendly Arcosaurans had left. Only a few Sauropods, a pack of Hadrodons and a couple other creatures remained. The Hadrodons did not stay for long. They seemed young and playful. Soon, their games took them out of sight. Then a Centuru squirmed its way back into the forest. The last of the Sauropods left them as they planned the next step in their journey.

Olena could still feel the ground shake from the giant Arcosauran's footsteps even though it was out of sight.

Karl said, "We've got a long walk ahead of us."

"Do we even know where we are going?" asked Kez.

"Or what to do when we get there?" added Olena.

"South and no, to answer you both," said Karl. "I'm a firm believer that things will happen, good or bad, the way they are supposed to."

Kez said, "South. Into some volcanic fields? I don't know exactly what that means, but I don't like the sound of it."

"The volcanic fields should be a desolate area where the ground is continuously erupting molten lava. As long as no one falls into a volcano, we should be fine," said Karl, seemingly unaware of the potential danger.

"Ka," said Olena. "Then what? Should we ask the Emperor nicely to turn the river back on and leave us alone?"

Olena wanted to have a definite plan. More than that though, she wanted to be back at Castle Empyrean so Fury could lead the Friesian Army down here. She did not know how many Carcharodans there were, but having her own army would make her feel much better.

Karl must have sensed her worry. He said, "We will restore the Brygos and stop Li-Am. The Forgotten Evil will not win this time."

This made Olena feel a little better. However, she did not like how Karl said *this time*. With the way he sometimes acted, she wondered if he knew of some other time that the Forgotten Evil might win.

They left the clearing with courage. The land did not seem too challenging for a walk beyond the huge cliff wall. They passed through groves of trees and climbed small hills. They saw no sign of the volcanic fields or any Arcosaurans.

In the late afternoon, the ground steadily rose away from them. The walk gradually turned into a climb. When they crested this hill, all signs of green vegetation remained behind them.

Olena stared at the emptiness, realizing they had now reached the volcanic fields. She could only see dull black rock continuing to the horizon. In some places the ground looked ripped apart from the inside and bright orange lava flowed out of the tears. Other than the lava, nothing else moved. Olena knew somewhere out there or beyond those fields, they would find Emperor Li-Am and the source of the Brygos River.

"This would be an excellent place to camp for the night," suggested Kez. "At least here we will still have some comfort. I expect very little softness awaiting us."

They spent the night on that ridge. Olena much preferred the soft grass over hard rock for a bed. As the sun set in the east, Olena scanned the desolation for any sign of life. She had no luck.

Then, with the last fading light, she spotted something. Olena spotted four tiny figures sailing low over the horizon. She suspected they were not Arcosaurans, but could not otherwise tell. The dark shapes came straight toward their small camp. Olena's vision zoomed in like it had on the balcony with Isis. That seemed like such a long time ago, but having another of her abilities work made her feel a little better. She also discovered the identity of their approaching visitors. It relieved her to see Captain Aeran and his other Guardian Hawks coming in for a landing.

Aeran spoke before he touched the ground, "Good evening, Your Majesty. Please, pardon the intrusion."

"You are quite welcome," said Olena, "but how did you know it was me?"

"You forget, I have eyes like a hawk," joked Aeran.

This made Olena laugh. Then she asked Kez to share some of their food with the miniature hawks. While they pecked at the large crumbs, they discussed recent events.

"Since we last saw you at the Hierakonpolis Marketplace," began Aeran.

Olena interrupted the Captain. He could not have known it was her because she wore the ring at the market. Ovara had been in control then.

"You did not see me at the marketplace," she said.

"Begging your pardon, we saw your advisors with another young lady. I assumed it was you using some type of glam," said Aeran. He cocked his head to the side, apparently waiting for an explanation.

Olena still thought it best to keep the ring a secret and offered nothing more.

Aeran continued, "At that time, we received word of a particular object being carried south."

"What object?" asked Kez.

The small bird hesitated.

"You can tell us," said Karl. "I believe it concerns the queen as well."

Again Karl seemed to know something impossible. How could he know what the birds were looking for? The four Guardians looked at each other and nodded in agreement. Aeran raised his head to swallow one last morsel of food.

"Where should I begin?" he asked himself. He quickly flicked his wings and shuddered, momentarily ruffling his chest feathers. "Well, your predecessor, the last Queen of the Eastern Sky, had a fascination with things that could fly. In particular, she loved all creatures with wings."

"I think I remember," said Olena.

"Had you seen what I am about to speak of, you would never forget," said Aeran.

She did remember, somewhat. The queen had a sleigh pulled by some large flying animals, recalled Olena. She could never forget the Alkonosts.

Kez said, "That's right. Twin Alkonosts."

"By far the most beautiful beings to ever grace the sky," said Aeran.

"I've heard of Alkonosts before," said Karl.

This did not surprise Olena.

He continued, "They are only female birds, but have human heads."

Aeran said, "And voices like nothing else that has ever existed. Their singing could bring peace to war and cause the stars to shine." He paused. "At least, that's how it felt."

"We heard them sing once, didn't we, Kez?" said Olena.

"Absolutely magnificent," said the quzzak. Olena saw the look on his face that matched the way she felt. Remembering the Alkonosts' singing made her feel like she was in a dream. The sound of their voices faintly rang in her ears.

"What happened?" asked Karl.

The hawk bowed his head. He said, "What happened was only my darkest day. I failed my mission which brought an end to the Queen of the Eastern Sky and the last two Alkonosts in existence."

Olena's mind went back to the wreckage. She remembered escaping Banookanook with Zandria and Kez. Running from the werewolves, they found the crashed sleigh and torn feathers. This brought back other sad memories. She thought about Banookanook and her father. Then she thought about being away from Zandria and losing her mother. So many bad things had happened since that day, yet so many amazing things happened as well.

Olena felt a sense of calm and hopefulness. Then she remembered that was the power of the Alkonosts. They could instill hope in any heart. She missed the Alkonosts.

"I never dared to hope again," said Aeran. "Then came the Rockhorn Battle and, after surviving that, time passed. Soon, I had a nest mate, Fleta. She is the most amazing hawk I have ever known."

One of the other birds, Olena thought his name was Habrok, cooed. They seemed to be teasing their captain.

Aeran continued, "As I was saying, Fleta brought me word of a rumor. With no chance of hope, I refused to believe in this impossibility. However, over the past several weeks, my trusted comrades and I have gathered evidence that proves the rumor true."

Karl looked excited as he said, "You found one?"

"It may be the only one," said Aeran, "but, yes, we found an Alkonost egg. If we do not fail, the Queen of the Eastern Sky may once again ride the wind."

"So, what are you doing here?" asked Kez.

"A wretched man known as Spynum Begg somehow came into possession of the egg."

"We know Spynum Begg," said Olena. "We're looking for him too."

"He probably did not even realize the value of what he had, but the man sold the egg to the creatures of this forsaken land. We believe he is personally carrying it to their Emperor. Unfortunately, we lost them through the jungle. We have backtracked several times with no luck."

Sylvan raised his spiked hand and pointed across the volcanic fields.

"Correct, my friend," said Kez. Then to Aeran, "What Sylvan means is that we have learned the Emperor is somewhere out there. We have to cross the volcanic fields."

The Captain excitedly flapped his wings. Olena thought he might fly away at any moment. Then he settled back to the ground.

"Then our paths cross once again, Your Majesty," said Captain Aeran. "We shall continue our journey together and escort you across these volcanic fields."

This made Olena feel somewhat better. Their party had doubled in size. She mused that if they met anyone else, they might end up with an army after all.

She slept uneasily, listening to the low rumble of the volcanoes in the distance.

Chapter 20

I don't like the risk, but I think you have to do it," said Kez. The queen and her two advisors sat away from Karl and the birds.

Sylvan nodded his big stone head in agreement. Olena confided in her two friends about using the Bronze Ring again. They agreed that she would be safer in disguise and that she should tell the others.

So, before they started into the volcanic fields that morning, Olena showed the ring to everyone. She briefly explained it to the four Guardian Hawks. She left out the part about possibly becoming trapped during this explanation.

The birds, Karl, Sylvan and Kez all watched as Olena slipped the ring onto her thumb for the third time.

As soon as she swirled through to the bronze room, Ogustus greeted her with a friendly smile and a big hug. She could not feel any of the emotion in his cold metal arms. Still, she appreciated the gesture. However, she wondered if it was only an act. She remembered Ogustus saying she would be tempted to return. While the Inhabitants continued to help her, something still made Olena think this might be an elaborate trap.

"It must be Omarika's turn," said Olena. She looked at the as yet unmoving statue of the tall woman.

"Always quick to action," said Ogustus. He rocked back on his chair. Olena thought he might fall off the back side. Then he leaned toward her. "In here, time does not move quite the same. We have the time to reacquaint ourselves while only an instant passes out there."

"Yeah, what's the rush?" added Ovara.

At least, Olena thought, this time Ovara did not try to scare her. However, she seemed to have the same unfriendly attitude as before.

"Ogustus knows," said Olena. "We have to stop Emperor Li-Am from invading the Southern Valley."

"Who's this Li-Am?" asked Ovara. Apparently, Ogustus did not share what happened to him the last time Olena wore the ring.

"He's the leader of the Arcosaurans who follow the Forgotten Evil," explained Olena.

Ovara said, "The Arcosaurans are a bedtime story. They're about as real as Immortals."

Olena did not want to have to explain everything again. She wished Ovara did not have to be so difficult. Before she said anything else, Omarika stepped down from her pedestal. This kept Olena from having to recount recent events.

The slender figure stepped between the girls and went straight for the mirror. Omarika had to duck slightly to clear the top of the frame. Then she slipped through the magic glass.

Looking through the murky portal, Olena could see her friends' surprise as Omarika appeared. It looked like Karl made introductions, but got no response from the mysterious woman.

"Tell me about her?" Olena asked Ogustus.

"That is very difficult for me," he said.

"She doesn't talk, remember?" said Ovara.

Olena remembered Ogustus said something about it before. She could not imagine that Omarika had not said a single word in the hundreds of years they had been together.

She understood this must be true and to confirm, asked, "You don't know anything about her?"

Ogustus nodded, solemnly. Then he smiled.

"I can tell you what I know about elves," said the big man. "She is an elf from our best guess. Maybe it will help."

Learning more about elves would be interesting, thought Olena. Other than Tym and

Dew, Olena did not know any others very well. She barely knew either of them. Olena guessed she would learn more about Omarika when she listened to her heart, but she did not want to connect with her completely unprepared.

The same as when Ogustus talked to her about Ovara, he settled onto his wide chair for the tale.

"Long before I was born, elves were much more powerful and more wild. They have always lived in caves, forests and across the Central Plains, very close with nature. In the beginning, they were much more careful about avoiding humans. During the First War for Empyrean, they agreed to fight on behalf of the First Queen. After that, they seemed to have much more tolerance for humans."

"You see, elves are the children of Immortals, so to speak. They gained their powers and long life from them. When the Immortals disappeared, the magic of the elves diminished. Their fighting skills did not, however. They could use every part of their body as a weapon. Some of their senses were enhanced by their magic. Some could see for miles, others could hear a feather hit the ground in Peckwood Forest all the way from their home in Truewood."

Olena knew those two forests were quite a long distance apart. She did not think she could hear something as quiet as a feather hitting the ground in the same room, let alone that far. She always knew elves were gifted, but never expected their true abilities. She wondered if Tym or Dew could do anything like that.

"For a short time, they lived with us humans. Again, before my time, they departed for more remote areas and have since kept their distance. They prefer a life of isolation."

Olena started to feel like she was sitting through one of Snow White's history lessons. She did not want to be rude, but believed she could learn more helpful things directly from Omarika.

"I think I am going to see where we're at," said Olena.

"I understand, liddel lady," said Ogustus. Then he froze back into a statue without another word.

Olena positioned herself in front of the mirror and closed her eyes. She did not immediately connect with Omarika. She almost had to struggle, like swimming up to the water's surface after a dive that went too deep.

As soon as she did connect with Omarika's heart, she discovered two things. First, that they had travelled quite a way into the volcanic fields, so much that she could no longer see the jungle or mountains behind them. Time really did move at a different speed in the bronze room. Secondly, she learned the truth about Omarika.

The elven woman had reasons for hiding her identity. This elf, like the other ring Inhabitants, lived a mostly good life ruined by a single bad decision. Also, like Ogustus, she served the queens of Empyrean. However, Omarika lived in Castle Empyrean.

Somehow, Omarika kept putting up mental blocks. Apparently, she did not want Olena to discover all of her secrets. Olena only caught glimpses of the always changing glass hallways of the familiar castle and flashes of an unknown battle.

Olena turned her attention to the volcanic fields. She had nothing interesting to see. The four hawks soared above them and they all kept their distance from any flowing lava. She could see from the sweat on Karl's face and shirt that it had become quite hot. Still, Omarika did not remove the turban that covered her face.

"Why do you keep your face hidden?" asked Olena in her head.

The answer came in the form of an image. She saw an angry Arcosauran swing its axe directly at her face. The muscular creature with its pointed snout and sharp teeth must have been a Carcharodan. Olena guessed this because he was as big as a Rockhorn and stood on two human-like legs. The image scared Olena. Apparently, Omarika tried to force Olena out of her head.

Olena refused to pull back and saw the rest of the vision. In this memory, Omarika blocked the swinging axe at the last second. Then she saw the Carcharodan's tail lash out and knock down another elf.

The vision seemed to freeze and Olena felt herself lift high into the sky. From her new perspective, she could see an enormous battle. Countless elves and Carcharodans fought fiercely across the great central plains.

Olena knew these plains well, but something was missing. Where Castle Empyrean should have been, she saw only the gaping mouth of the bottomless canyon. On the southern edge, she spotted a wide river spilling in a magnificent waterfall into the canyon. That must be the Brygos, she thought. Then a gigantic hawk swooped in front of her vision. This brought Olena back to the present.

The hawk from Omarika's memory looked like the same breed as Captain Aeran, only about fifty times bigger. Olena looked up at the tiny hawks in the sky. Omarika seemed to have no problem keeping a tireless pace with the swift birds, while the others started to fall behind. She worried that Ogustus would not have been able to handle this terrain. That made her somewhat happier to be with Omarika right now.

She wanted to know more about this strange elf. These memories must be of the First War for Empyrean, Olena thought. She knew elves lived a long time, but this meant Omarika could be as old as Empyrean itself. She must have known the first queens if she spent time at Castle Empyrean. Olena fought against Omarika's mental blocks to see more of her memories.

"Why do you pry?" thought Omarika.

This stunned Olena. She had never heard the elf's voice and did not expect it. Even in her head, the secretive woman spoke in a whisper.

Olena quickly recovered from the shock and answered, "If I can learn why you are trapped in the ring, maybe I can help you get out. Maybe I can keep myself from getting trapped too."

"Then know this," thought Omarika.

The elf must have decided to trust Olena and allowed her to see another memory.

This time, Omarika walked the halls of Castle Empyrean. Olena understood from Omarika that she did not serve at the castle until the reign of the Second Queen of the Northern Wood, several hundred years after the First War for Empyrean. She also understood that at this time, all four queens had mysteriously disappeared.

Omarika headed to the throne room with her young son at her side. It surprised Olena to discover the child to be Tym. Olena's reaction to Tym caused the memory to stop immediately before they entered the room to meet the strange girl known as the Passing Queen.

"I had forgotten my son," thought Omarika.

"He is a good friend," responded Olena. Olena wanted to see the Passing Queen, but Omarika's thoughts shifted to her son.

"My son has aged well since I've been gone. The love you have for him in your heart has awakened something in mine. You must know the rest," thought Omarika.

The next memory took place not long after Omarika met the Passing Queen for the first time. Olena still did not see this queen with which she shared some of her abilities. Omarika loved her son Tym dearly and thought her actions would protect him. She let Olena know that the Passing Queen had the Bronze Ring. Omarika believed it to have evil powers and decided to steal it in order to protect the Passing Queen.

She did not show Olena the whole memory, but Omarika let her know that was how she became trapped in the ring.

"My efforts were in vain because the Passing Queen did use the ring even after my sacrifice. We then decided together to hide my identity as we thought it would protect Tym from the shame of my treason. Attempting to steal the ring went very badly and it was better that everyone thought I died then," thought Omarika.

"You don't have to hide anymore," said Olena. She felt sorry for Omarika and wanted to reunite her with her son. "He is highly trusted and very honorable. Please take off your mask."

Omarika slowly unraveled her turban and felt the sun on her pale face for the first time in hundreds of years. She shook out her silky blond hair and it hung down her back almost to her knees. She examined her travelling companions with her pure white eyes.

"Malika Lantisphere? Is that you?" asked Karl.

"She is my twin sister," whispered Omarika.

"That makes better sense," said Karl.

"Why are you still whispering?" thought Olena.

"I will show you one other thing, then please let my memories sleep," Omarika thought back.

"I promise," agreed Olena.

She saw the battlefield again. It still looked strange with a river and no crystal castle. The twin sisters of the Lantisphere clan stood back to back, surrounded by a hoard of Carcharodans. The one with silky blond hair and white eyes was unmistakably Omarika and the one with midnight black hair and matching eyes had to be Malika. During this battle, Ogustus' words about elven abilities came back to Olena. She learned Omarika's power was not in her hearing or sight, but in her voice.

As the ferocious Arcosaurans charged, Omarika yelled, "Be gone!"

The shockwave from her mouth disintegrated the first row of Carcharodans. As the sound carried, forty or fifty more attackers flew through the air. At an unbelievable distance, several hundreds more were knocked to the ground. The elf continued to use her voice to knock back foes, but it took all of her strength to yell like that and could only do it so powerfully once before having to rest her voice for ten or twenty years.

Olena now understood the destructive power of Omarika's voice and why she chose to only whisper. If Ogustus was correct, Omarika should not be as powerful now, but her scream may still be quite dangerous.

As promised, Olena did not pry into any more of Omarika's memories. She felt like she had already learned a lot about her. They continued across the volcanic fields with a new understanding of each other.

While the group tried to avoid the lava, one time a new crack formed almost at their feet. The ground suddenly became soft and moved in waves like the ocean. Then unbelievably hot lava seeped out of the ground. A large bubble of it popped and a glob flew straight at Kez.

Omarika moved so fast that Olena could not even see her. The elf flipped, grabbed Kez while she was upside down and landed on her feet, safely clear of the deadly lava.

"I thank you for saving my life," said Kez.

Omarika simply nodded.

The rest of the group moved carefully around the cauldron. No one wanted to find out how hot it actually was.

Finally, after what seemed like too long, they neared the large volcanoes. Mountains surrounded them on both sides. Olena asked Omarika to lead them toward the highest mountain and Karl agreed.

"That would be the most likely place for an army to hide," said Karl.

Between the rocky crags and steep ledges, Olena lost sight of the Guardian Hawks. Then the one she thought was called Bellevue found them.

"Your Majesty, we have found something you should see," said Bellevue.

The small bird led them from their present path through a narrow crevasse. When they turned a sharp corner, the four hawks perched above them. There, Olena saw the first living being they had met since entering the volcanic fields.

"Definitely not an Arcosauran," said Kez.

The pathetic creature maybe came up to Olena's knees. It looked like a cross between a large snail and a spider. However, it only had four spindly legs poking out of holes on the top of its shell. They looked too thin to support its body or lift it off the ground, but it did. It used two blue stalks on its face as feelers, searching its way along the pass. Maybe it's blind, thought Olena. Then she noticed a jagged crack on the creature's shell. Green puss oozed from the infected wound.

"Who's there?" asked the snail. It sounded to Olena like he had a mouth full of jelly. Every word came out of his mouth sounding gooey and accompanied by dripping slime.

"We're friends," said Karl. "And you?"

"Lost," said the snail. "I sense you travel with one of my old Rockhorn." Olena wondered how he could tell they had a Rockhorn with them. "For that reason I think I can trust you. I have been wandering these lands for almost a year in search of an old friend."

Already, Olena did not like this creature. She could not imagine why being with a Rockhorn would make them more trustworthy. With the exception of Sylvan, the only Rockhorns that anyone else knew were evil.

Kez said, "You're not likely to find anyone out here. Who is this friend?"

The blind creature replied, "He is the Emperor of Arcenland."

Now it made sense. This creature knew of Rockhorns and considered Li-Am a friend. That evil Carcharodan only had friends like Spynum Begg. This gave Olena a solid idea of the snail's identity.

"What's your name?" Olena asked with a whisper through Omarika's mouth.

The snail stood as tall as it could, like a soldier puffing out its chest. Two claws poked out from under its body, the left damaged beyond use. It used its sharp right claw to preen its eye stalks.

"I am General Gusk."

Olena could feel the shock from the group. She thought Karl already knew the answer though. Everyone knew Gusk's name except Omarika. Olena quickly showed her memories of the Rockhorn Battle and the fact that Gusk disappeared before being captured. Omarika wanted to respond by smashing Gusk, but Olena asked her not to. If Gusk got his idea for the Rockhorn Army from the Carcharodans, maybe he knew where they lived. Between his blindness and severe shell injury, he must have been having a difficult time finding his way there. She wondered if he had been wandering aimlessly for the past year.

Instead of letting Omarika crush him, she spoke through the elf to Karl. "Maybe we can help each other find his friend?"

"Oh, I suspect so. We are in the presence of greatness and should do what we can to ensure he is reunited," said Karl. He must have understood what Olena felt. She did not think it would be wise to reveal their identity or purpose to the snail.

Gusk chewed out, "If only we could find the Brygos River. The Emperor's home is at its source. Sadly, I think it flows underground in this land. If only we had a way to see into the tops of the volcanoes."

Aeran, Derek, Bellevue and Habrok took to the air without a word.

By the time Omarika and Karl led General Gusk out of the crevasse, Derek returned.

"We have found it," said the hawk. Olena breathed a sigh of relief that he did not call her Your Majesty. "As we thought, our destination is in the largest of the mountains."

It took some time, but eventually, they made it to the rim of the tallest and widest of the volcanoes in Arcenland. Olena did not know what to expect when they looked over the edge.

A sheer drop of thousands of feet greeted her. The inside of the volcano was completely hollow. The ground they stood on could only have been a shell of a few feet thick. The possibility of falling terrified Olena and she asked Omarika to move away from the edge. She had a weakness for heights ever since she almost fell from the balcony the day she became queen.

Before moving back to a safe distance, Olena had a view of the sprawling city. At one end, she saw a huge lake that must have been the source of the Brygos. On the other end, she saw a fortified palace. Between them, she saw an enormous lake of lava and a huge layered structure that blocked the flow of the river.

In the brief glimpse before her stomach churned, Olena could barely take in all of the sights. She feared she would be there soon enough to observe all the details. For now, she realized that this apparently dormant volcano was home to an entire race that had supposedly gone extinct. She did not dare to peek back over the ledge. The massiveness of their city both impressed her and terrified her. She felt anger and some fear from Omarika. It had been a long time since she thought about the Carcharodans.

Karl did not appear to have the same paralyzing fear of heights.

Still looking over the edge, he said, "They built a dam. We have to find a way down there."

Chapter 21

Away from the dizzying drop, Olena took time to think of a plan. She did not know why her plan would be any better than Karl or Kez's, but something gave her an idea. Maybe it had to do with her abilities as a queen, she thought.

"Olena wants to remain in disguise," whispered Omarika. She explained Olena's plan to Karl, Kez, Sylvan and Captain Aeran. None of them knew how well General Gusk could hear, so they moved down the slope as he slowly navigated his way toward them. The other three hawks pecked at pebbles near the snail for an added distraction.

It made Olena feel funny to travel with Gusk. She knew he was evil. He made no attempt to hide his feelings. As long as the others kept her secret, she thought maybe they could use Gusk to get into Li-Am's palace.

"But what do we do once we're inside?" asked Kez.

"That's when we split up," said Omarika.

Olena saw a look of surprise on everyone's face, except Karl's. Even Captain Aeran seemed concerned.

"We can't do that," said Kez. Sylvan also shook his stone head from side to side, meaning no.

Karl, looking satisfied with the plan already, said, "Everything happens the way it's supposed to."

"It's not safe for Olena," demanded Kez.

Omarika laid out the rest of the plan, "Kez, you and Sylvan have the most important task. You must go north immediately and bring back as much help as you can."

"The Parasauratitan already said they won't help." Obviously, Kez did not want to leave.

"Then you have to get back to Hierakonpolis," whispered Omarika. "Or even all the way to Castle Empyrean, if you have to. Karl and I will remain hidden and try to find a way to open the dam or maybe destroy it. Without control of the Brygos, Li-Am will have to listen to us."

Kez stopped walking and folded his arms. He said, "I don't like it. My place is with Olena."

"The best help you can be to her now is to bring back an army before Li-Am starts his invasion," said Karl.

"What of us, milady?" asked Aeran. He seemed eager to do anything.

"The Guardian Hawks must complete their quest. No matter what else happens, find the Alkonost egg. That will bring hope and strength to the people of Empyrean," said Omarika.

"We will go at once," said the tiny Captain. He flew from his perch on Karl's shoulder and joined his comrades near Gusk. Without saying anything, the birds took wing. After a moment's conversation high out of earshot, the four birds flew off over the top of the mighty volcano.

Gusk finally caught up with them. "So many whispers," he said. "What devious thing are you planning my new friends?"

Karl spoke with quick thinking, "We did not want to offend you, General. We worried with your old injury if we should offer to carry you."

The idea of picking up the slimy evil creature made Olena feel like she might lose her breakfast. Still, she knew Karl only said it to hide their true plan.

"That is not necessary. I still have my honor," said Gusk. "Besides, it will not be long before we are in Emperor Li-Am's court, where I will be healed."

They continued down the slope, making their way toward the rocky crags near where the rocks looked water worn. Olena saw many cracks and holes. She guessed when the Brygos flowed from the mountain, it washed out here before continuing north underground. Close to the bottom of the volcano, Olena urged Omarika to send Kez and Sylvan on their mission.

Sylvan seemed to accept his instructions. However, Kez still refused. He stayed on the ground well out of Sylvan's reach.

"Nothing could force me to leave your side," stated Kez.

Then something whooshed by them on an overhead ledge. Small rocks dropped down, but whatever it was made no other sound. Another whoosh came behind them. Olena could not tell if more than one thing surrounded them.

One of the shapes came down the slope and disappeared around the next corner of the narrow pass. Olena spotted what looked like a bundle of dirty rags. She heard a brief flutter of the cloth in the wind and then nothing.

The party stopped, waiting silently.

Gusk said, "This is unfortunate. I'm afraid the Jindig have found us."

"What are Jindig?" asked Karl.

Olena could not believe that they encountered something that he did not know, but they found out an instant later. A creature that looked like the skeleton of a dog wrapped in dirty rags leapt seemingly out of nowhere. It landed on Gusk and the two of them rolled down the path. Its sharp teeth gnawed at Gusk's cracked shell.

Then another Jindig landed on Sylvan's back. Karl spotted three more sliding down the mountainside directly toward them. Their clothes trailed behind them like capes in the wind. Their jaws snapped open and closed, while the empty eye sockets of their skulls somehow still looked mad.

Suddenly, two Arcosaurans, as big as Sylvan's Rockhorn, appeared from around the corner. Olena guessed there must be caves all through this area to allow entrance to the volcano. She instantly realized these two must be Carcharodans and they looked more horrible than she imagined.

The monsters had bodies like huge men and walked on two legs. Small plates of armor, strapped on with leather, covered their chest and shoulders. Orange, almost yellow, scales covered their bodies from their pointed noses to the tips of the tails dangling behind them. With his protruding jaw hanging open, Olena could see double rows of sharp teeth on both the top and bottom of one of the Carcharodan's mouths. Both Arcosaurans stared at the scene with beady eyes set back under a thick brow.

Olena felt a rush of memories flood Omarika's heart. She thought briefly about the First War for Empyrean and fighting endlessly against these creatures. However, mostly she missed her son and her sister.

The Carcharodans attacked the Jindig. The meaner-looking of the two soldiers snatched Gusk and his Jindig from the ground. He pulled the Jindig off of the snail and threw it. The frightening skeleton vanished and the rags flew apart, falling empty to the ground. The Carcharodan finished by slurping Gusk out of his shell. He ate the wicked General in one bite. The cracked shell looked small in the Carcharodan's four, clawed-fingers. As he chewed the last of General Gusk, the huge monster tossed the empty shell over his shoulder. The other Jindig quickly scattered as the Arcosaurans turned on Karl and Omarika.

Fear held Omarika in place. Olena realized it had been so long since the elf faced any Carcharodans. She could feel the terror in Omarika's heart. The monsters frightened her too, but she needed the elf to move or they might easily end up like Gusk.

The second Carcharodan's slobbering jaws came down toward Omarika's head. She still could not move. At the last possible moment, a huge stone club knocked the beast back.

Sylvan attacked the vicious Arcosaurans.

Olena watched the fight in amazement. She never expected Sylvan to be capable of such a feat.

It looked almost like a dance. Sylvan's Rockhorn body spun and twisted. He ducked and dodged all of the strikes from the Carcharodan's claws and tails. Her friend repeatedly landed blow after blow with both his club hand and his spear hand. She watched him spin backward, while his feet faced forward, and smash one of the beasts in the face. Several razor-like teeth flew through the air.

The fight did not last nearly as long as it seemed. Sylvan ended it with a tremendous uppercut to the bottom jaw of the second

Carcharodan. Although slightly smaller than both Arcosaurans, Sylvan won the fight. He left both creatures unmoving on the ground.

"Fantastic," shouted Karl.

For a moment, Olena thought Omarika's heart stopped beating. Then it pounded hard. Olena felt a surge of strength and anger in the elf.

"I can never apologize enough," thought Omarika. "That will never happen again."

"It's okay. I understand," Olena thought back to her. She did understand. Olena understood that Omarika did not want to share her fear with the others. She also understood the elf probably had not seen a Carcharodan for hundreds, maybe thousands, of years. When she last did, they were mortal enemies.

Kez quickly scrambled up to Sylvan's shoulder. "I think I understand this situation better now. Perhaps, Sylvan and I should go for reinforcements."

"That would be helpful," said Karl. "I'm going to find the cave these two crawled out of." Karl walked off around the corner ahead of them.

Omarika stood alone with Sylvan and Kez. Olena asked her to repeat something.

Omarika whispered, "I need you to know I love you both. I want to thank you now for going to get help in case I don't get another chance."

"Don't say that," said Kez. He looked on the verge of tears as he said, "You will assuredly have the opportunity to thank us later."

Thankful that Kez did not cry, Olena broke her connection with Omarika. She sat alone in the bronze room and started crying. Seeing her friend in tears would have only made things more difficult.

Olena did not know what was going to happen and that scared her. For her friends' sake, she did not want them to see her like this. She hoped Ogustus and Ovara were not watching her either from their statue forms. She knew a Queen of Empyrean was not supposed to show fear.

When she reconnected with Omarika, the elf followed Karl through a narrow cave. Glowing mushrooms clinging to the walls and ceiling lit their path. When they exited the tunnel, they stood on one end of the long dam inside the giant volcano.

Olena looked across the lake, twice the size of the Nata Playa, which she recalled from when she first entered the Southern Valley. On the other side of the dam, she watched a narrow stream of water spill out into a deep, black hole. This must be where the Brygos River starts its underground journey to the Abydos in Hierakonpolis, she guessed. She could not believe how much Li-Am robbed from the people of the Southern Valley.

"If only I had some pyroagitating powder, that would be something," said Karl. He searched his satchel, with no luck. "We need to find a way to blow up this thing."

Olena did not know exactly what he meant by blow up, but she knew Karl had an exceptional talent for making things fall apart. Although clumsy and sometimes strange, she really grew to trust him over the past several days. She could think of very few other people that she could or would want to rely on at a time like this.

At the far end of the dam, Olena spotted several smaller, more human-looking Arcosaurans. She guessed them to be the green Baharians and warned Omarika. The elf tapped Karl on the shoulder to show him the approaching danger. She did not think her friends had been spotted yet.

When they turned to go back into hiding, a squad of four Carcharodans blocked their escape.

Chapter 22

Heading back across the volcanic fields proved easier than the first passing. Sylvan did not have to slow his pace for anyone. Kez could barely hold on at the incredible speed that Sylvan could move the long Rockhorn legs. Wind whipped Kez's face and kept his tail furled out behind him like a flag.

The whole time, Kez could only think about Olena. He wished he could have seen her face one more time. Instead, he had to say goodbye to a quiet elf.

Now every second they wasted might decide that little girl's fate. He cared for her because she was the Queen of the Eastern Sky, but more so because she was his friend.

Kez spent so much time thinking about playing on the beach with Olena and Zandria. He missed those days. In a way, he almost felt like a father to her. His own offspring had grown and they had quzzies of their own. He watched her grow and had so many good memories. However, he looked forward to all of the possibilities of their new life. He did not want that to be over before it barely started.

With unbelievable speed, they crossed the volcanic fields in less than half a day. One time, Sylvan stepped in a newly formed lava pot. Kez felt the heat almost singe his fur. Sylvan suffered no real damage however. Kez expected the stone legs to melt like the rest of the rock around it. Either through the dark magic of its original creation or Karl's binding alchemy, the Rockhorn suffered no other damage than having its tan legs turn black from the charring.

Back in the Arcenland jungle, Kez's thoughts turned to his last visit to his home jungle. He remembered wishing for his own adventure. He wanted to do something important. At the time, he resigned his fate to more peaceful plans. Now, he found himself in a situation he never could have imagined. He did get his wish and Kez proudly shared it with Sylvan.

Through the strange trees, they saw the occasional Sauropod and a few playful Hadrodons. Kez decided their first best option would be to plead with the Parasauratitan for help, if they could find him.

Kez remembered being angry with the Parasauratitan. The old Arcosauran refused to help them before. With the new information of the dam, the quzzak hoped the Immortal would reconsider.

As they sped along, Kez spotted the three Trisariens in their path, like they had been waiting for them. He tapped Sylvan's head to get him to stop. It relieved Kez to find them. He thought they might be more sympathetic than the other Arcosaurans. Besides, he enjoyed talking to beautiful women at any time.

The ink covered leader of the females stepped forward. Kez looked at the exquisite designs on her arms and legs. She looked like a work of art.

"We know why you return," she said. "The elder has made his decision. We Trisariens wish we could help, but the others fear it would mean our own extinction."

"But you're all in danger already," said Kez. "Don't you realize Li-Am will find you all eventually?"

"That may be true, but the Parasauratitan feels there may be a resolution without our intervention," said the Trisarien. "We will continue the debate on your behalf, but I recommend you continue toward Empyrean to seek assistance."

With that, the Trisariens walked into the jungle and disappeared. Kez felt hopeless now. He believed Hierakonpolis to be too far. What if everyone refused them there as well, he thought. He recalled Horus already saying they would not go to war.

Sylvan did not wait for Kez to say anything. He began running north again. Within a short time, they stood on the edge of the Unending Desert. The thought of helpful Arcosaurans faded with the jungle behind them.

"How quickly do you think you can cross it?" asked Kez.

Sylvan shrugged his shoulders and then he pointed at the horizon. A familiar figure approached them. Kez did not think the desert guardian Phix could help them, but at least he would ask.

Phix started speaking when he came close. "You have already been granted safe passage. You do not need to wait for me in order to cross."

Kez said, "The Queen of the Eastern Sky is in trouble. We may have a chance to stop Li-Am and his army, but we need help."

"I am but one creature and my fate is with the Unending Desert. I will fight against anything that threatens my land, but I cannot leave the sand beneath my feet," said Phix.

"Isn't there anything you can do?" pleaded Kez. "We need to go north, not back to the jungle."

The man with the lion's body thought for a moment.

"I believe I can carry you and your friend to Hierakonpolis. My desert sand blows on the streets of that great city. It has been too long since I walked those avenues. Climb on my back and I will have you there in the blink of an eye."

As they mounted Phix, Kez did not realize they were already too late.

Chapter 23

The Baharians almost scared Olena more than the Carcharodans. Their flat, lipless faces and green scales made them seem very sinister. They both had too many frightening weapons though.

The two groups of Arcosaurans led Omarika and Karl through the city toward the palace. Despite being an evil place, the city looked beautiful. Olena marveled at the architecture. Huge archways and wide streets could easily allow Sauropods to roam the city. Most everything looked carved out of the stone inside the mountain. They had two and three-story buildings with winding staircases. On one side of the city, the buildings reached even higher up the sides of the volcano and looked to have bridges and walkways between them. Olena tried to picture a time when the streets could have been crowded with every type of Arcosauran.

In the center of the city, they crossed a huge bridge suspended over a roiling cauldron of lava. Olena wondered how they kept this small lake of fire from erupting and destroying their city. The lava seemed angry, if that was possible. She guessed some magic held it back.

This bridge led to a walled complex that had to be Li-Am's palace. As they passed through the front gate, Olena saw hundreds of Carcharodan and Baharian soldiers training for the impending invasion in the courtyard.

Eventually, they made it through the cave like halls to the throne room. Li-Am sat on a chair in the middle of the room that appeared to be made from the skull of a Sauropod. The Emperor himself had to be the biggest of all Carcharodans. Olena thought he could be at least a full head taller than any other Carcharodan she had seen so far in this city. The armor on his shoulders differed from the others in that it had three metal spikes on each shoulder. He also had a gold band around the tip of his tail covered with spikes. His crown looked rather simple, however. It looked like a metal headband with a wingtip on the back of each side and a point pressing down the center slope of his forehead. It surprised Olena that it was so plain when Li-Am appeared to be a ruler of extravagance.

The wretched Spynum Begg stood to the left of the throne. He appeared to have been rewarded well for his evil deeds. Olena did not remember him being dressed so well or adorned with as much jewelry as he currently had.

It actually relieved Olena to see him here. She did not know what was going to happen, but she wanted Begg to be present when it did. She believed he had to pay for his crimes.

The Baharian guards forced Karl and Omarika onto their knees in front of the Emperor. Olena did not expect things to happen this way. She never truly had a plan, but this seemed like the worst possible outcome.

"You are from the Southern Valley of Empyrean," growled Li-Am. It came out somewhat as a question, but more like a statement, as if he assumed the answer.

Olena would not have answered, but Karl said, "We are."

"Now you trespass with such audacity," said Li-Am. "And you bring one of these...these things with you." Apparently, Li-Am felt the same toward elves as Omarika felt about Carcharodans.

Karl said, "I would not call it trespassing per say. I think we took a wrong turn somewhere. Then I heard you had a really good restaurant downtown."

"Silence!" demanded the Emperor. "You think to make me laugh, but you are not so funny when you see how we deal with trespassers."

Li-Am nodded to one of the Baharians who drew a sword with a very jagged edge. Olena screamed at Omarika to move. She at least wanted her to fight back if the end was near.

Omarika thought, "It will only bring more suffering to your friends if I resist now." Then the elf used her mental abilities to sever their connection.

Olena opened her eyes in the bronze room. She immediately turned to the mirror to see what happened. A black cloud shrouded the mirror and she could see nothing. Omarika blocked her completely.

"It's not fair. You have to do what I say," cried Olena.

Ogustus and Ovara quickly moved to her side. Ovara did not look very worried, but Ogustus seemed concerned.

"You don't know all the rules yet, so you're not in control," gloated Ovara.

"Liddel lady, we will help when we can, but now is not the time," said Ogustus.

"I have to help them. I have to tell Li-Am who I am," said Olena.

"What good will it do for him to know you are an Empyrical Queen?" asked Ovara.

"I don't know, but I have to tell the truth," said Olena.

Ogustus smiled with his normal broad expression when she came up with the correct answer. "Ah, then you have learned the fourth rule, always tell the truth."

Suddenly, the mirror sucked in Olena and she traded places with Omarika. She saw the Baharian sword swinging straight toward her head.

"Tawakafa," ordered Li-Am. He gave the southern order to stop with only a second to spare.

The Baharian stopped his weapon only inches from her neck.

Olena eeked out a tiny, "Ka."

"Who are you?" asked Li-Am.

Before she could answer, Spynum Begg offered, "She is Queen of the Eastern Sky, Your Exaltedness."

Li-Am bent down low. Olena could feel his hot breath on her face. "Is this true?"

"Yes. I am Olena, Queen of the Eastern Sky of Empyrean. I bring only my breath from which all things start anew and with it I demand you open the Brygos River." She did not know if her words would do anything, but it was the most powerful magical saying she knew.

Li-Am leaned back quickly. Olena could not tell if it was fear or surprise, but her words did get to him. She suspected he was not afraid of her though. She must have surprised him by speaking so boldly. Most likely, he was not used to being talked to like that.

"You are in no position to make demands," said Li-Am. Several of the surrounding Arcosaurans chuckled at her expense. "However, your courage intrigues me. I have a task for you."

"I will submit to your task, if you release the river," said Olena in her most regal voice.

"Then prepare the Spinolock," Li-Am ordered his attendants.

Karl jumped up and said, "No, wait. She can't do that." Then to Olena, "You can't do that." He turned back to Li-Am, "This is not possible. I have it on good authority that Spinolocks are extinct."

"Not this one," laughed Li-Am. "Take them away until it is time."

Several Baharians dragged Olena and Karl from the room. They continued down several flights of stairs and long halls until they ended up in a dungeon cell. One of the guards locked the door and then they were alone.

"This is not good," complained Karl. "You really shouldn't have agreed to his task, especially without knowing what it was."

"What is a Spinolock?" asked Olena.

Karl said, "Only the biggest and most voracious of all Arcosaurans, bigger than a Sauropod. The thing could eat a Carcharodan in one bite and that would be an appetizer. It sounds like they have one for a pet."

"Maybe Kez will bring help," Olena said.

With another of his prophetic statements, Karl said, "They don't make it in time." He seemed sure of this, like he already knew the outcome. Before Olena could ask him how he knew, his eyes got wide. "These walls are made from the key ingredient in pyroagitating powder. I have everything else in my pouch to make us some powder."

Olena looked at the stone. It did not look any different from any other she had seen, but he thought it was special. The boy immediately began chipping at the wall with another rock, knocking small pieces onto the floor. Olena did not expect to get another response from him, so she turned her attention to the Bronze Ring. Maybe the Inhabitants could help her, she thought. Olena slipped the ring onto her thumb.

In the bronze room, all three Inhabitants greeted her, eagerly waiting. She learned their rules, but still did not feel in control. She hoped they had an idea or maybe a way to escape.

"You know the rules, yes?" asked Ogustus.

"I think so," answered Olena.

"Please, tell us," he said.

Olena thought for a moment, standing in the middle of the bronze room with her back to the magic mirror. Finally, she said, "First, listen to your heart. Then, have faith and trust yourself. And even if it means trouble for you, always tell the truth."

"Excellent good work," beamed Ogustus. "Do you realize these words apply not only to your secret ring, but also to your life? All of the power and magic you need to overcome anything dwells in your own heart. Follow these rules and you shall never be defeated."

At that moment, it occurred to Olena that her problems came from self doubt. If she truly believed in these rules, maybe her magic would work. It felt like so long ago, when she sat at Castle Empyrean, bored of her lessons. If she knew these things then, she never would have been in this position. Of course, she never would have met Karl or the Inhabitants either.

"Don't let us down," said Ovara, "and we'll be there for you. Now get back out there."

Olena took off the ring and found herself back in the cell with Karl. He acted like he did not notice her missing a moment before. What felt like a long conversation in the bronze room must have only lasted an instant out here.

"Okay, I have plenty of pyroagitating powder to make enough fireworks for three Queen's Days. I wanted to tell you about something else though."

"Karl, I think we are going to get out of this," she said.

"Oh, I know. That's why I need to tell you about my portal. It's not exactly like your Walking Portal. I have to make a few designs and say a chant to get it going, then we step right through to wherever we want to go. In theory, we could travel in time or maybe even another dimension."

A Baharian guard interrupted them by opening the cell door. Two more guards grabbed them and roughly ushered them out of the cell.

They pushed Karl out in front and dragged Olena behind them. He turned over his shoulder to finish with, "Don't worry, I've used it successfully." Among the grunting and hustling of the guards, Olena did not hear him add, "Almost."

The guards did not take them back to the throne room. Instead, at the end of another long hallway, they took Karl up a flight of stairs. The guards then led Olena to a steel door. They opened it and shoved her through, closing and locking the door behind her.

Olena found herself on a dirt field surrounded by high walls. One of the walls looked like a massive gate. On the opposite side from the door she came through, Olena saw Emperor Li-Am sitting in an observation box at the top of the wall. Spynum Begg stood on one side of him and Karl Lumpkin was on the other, held by guards.

The Emperor spoke, "Your task is simple. Solve the maze before the Spinolock catches you."

Hundreds of Carcharodans and Baharians cheered from countless rows of benches above her. Olena realized they must be surrounding the maze, along the high walls. Olena thought this must be a great spectacle for them.

Then the massive gate opened to reveal a second gate made of steel bars. Through the bars, Olena saw the most horrifying of all Arcosaurans. Like Karl said, the Spinolock looked taller than a Sauropod, but it stood on two thick legs, instead of four. Its front two limbs did not look long enough to even be considered arms. A huge sail spanned the length of the creature's back. The long narrow head worried Olena the most. When the Spinolock roared, she thought its open mouth had plenty of room to fit her completely in one bite while sitting on Fury's back.

Her first instinct made Olena try her Walking Portal, but nothing happened. Despite her new found confidence, her magic did not seem to be restored.

Then Olena noticed the second gate move up slightly. It clicked into place like rising on some sort of timer. With each notch, her time was wasting. At the second notch, the Spinolock started to look anxious.

On the fourth wall, Olena spotted a small pattern of blocks positioned slightly above her head. It looked like a puzzle, but the symbols must have been in an Arcosauran language that she did not know how to read. Olena remembered that Ogustus was an expert at solving puzzles. She quickly popped the Bronze Ring on her thumb.

Like with her Walking Portal, nothing happened. Olena did not change into Ogustus, she did not swirl away to the bronze room. She started to feel panicked.

"Doan worry liddel lady," said Ogustus. Olena could feel him in her heart and hear his voice in her head. "This is simple mathematics, a child's game."

Olena looked at the nine blocks on the wall. She studied the three rows, each with three symbols. Still, they made no sense to her.

"We only have to reposition them so that each row and column has the same sum," Ogustus said.

"But I don't know what a sum is," Olena said aloud. "Besides, I can't even read them."

Ogustus responded, "Trust yourself and let me guide you."

Almost out of reach, Olena stood on her tiptoes to move the blocks according to Ogustus' guidance. When she placed the last block, she heard a loud click and the wall slid down into the ground. The true maze began on the other side. Olena looked back to see the bars now raised high enough for the Spinolock to barely squeeze its snapping jaws under it. It craned its neck and roared out at her.

Olena ran into the maze.

She did not know if Ogustus could help her any longer and wanted to connect with Ovara. After the winding streets and back alleys of Hierakonpolis, she trusted the girl's sense of direction. Olena thought maybe by spinning the ring on her thumb, she might change Inhabitants. She had no idea if that would work, but it felt right.

Upon twisting the ring, she instantly connected with Ovara. The southern girl told her which way to turn at each intersection. Ovara clearly had a knack for this as they did not go down one dead end or make a single wrong turn. Ovara navigated the maze as easily as Tym navigated the constantly changing halls of Castle Empyrean. Olena did not have the time to wonder why Ovara was so good at this.

After many twists and turns, Olena found herself at a stopping point. With the obstacle in front of her, she did not think she could go on any further. In the distance, Olena could see the backside of Li-Am's observation box. She had come full circle while the Emperor, Spynum Begg and Karl watched her the whole time. Between her and the apparent end of the maze remained the final obstacle. Hot lava bubbled up from a deep chasm. The only way across seemed to be a spider web of narrow beams interspersed with jabbing spikes and spinning blades.

"I can help," came Omarika's whisper as Olena turned the ring on her thumb once more. She knew the elf had the acrobatic skill to make it across, but doubted if Omarika could help her move her own small body. A horrendous roar jangled Olena's nerves.

Karl yelled, "The gate's open. The Spinolock is coming through the maze!"

Olena did not hesitate any longer. She walked out on the narrow beam that was not even as wide as her foot. She held her arms out to her sides for balance and resisted the urge to look below her.

The first beam went straight across and Olena thought she could make it easy. A spinning blade forced her to jump to a different beam. Olena almost lost her balance now looking down at the molten rock. She had the strange sensation of Omarika holding her, keeping her steady. She looked around to see she was alone on the beam.

She followed this beam up to the right. A sharp spike met her at the end, poking repeatedly at her from here. Olena had no choice but to jump to another beam. As soon as she landed, another blade came at her. On instinct, probably Omarika's instinct, she did an aerial somersault over the blade and grabbed a higher beam with her hands.

Dangling for a moment, Olena pulled herself up and looked around the web. She now rested at the highest point in the center of the chasm.

The Spinolock appeared from the maze in all of its horrific magnificence. Slobber dripped from teeth as long as her arm. It stopped, possibly examining the mesh of beams and blades. Could it be scared of the lava, wondered Olena. The Spinolock came up to the edge of the chasm and roared at Olena, its head even with hers while it stood on the ground and she stood at the top.

Luckily, she was slightly out of reach. Olena tried to ignore the giant monster, fighting fear and concentrating on Omarika. Together, they crossed the remainder of the web with a little elven style and growing confidence. She thanked Omarika in her head when they made it to solid ground. She now stood in another dead end, like the one at the start of the maze, with no apparent exit.

With the Spinolock safely blocked from her, Olena shouted at Li-Am, "I completed your task, now let us go."

The Emperor roared, "I never agreed to your demands." Then he pushed a lever at his side. The blades and spikes over the pit retracted and the beams began slowly lowering. They folded down one by one and started to resemble a bridge. Olena realized it would only be a matter of moments before the Spinolock could reach her.

Olena had nowhere to go. She could not find a door on this side or climb the smooth walls. She looked to Karl for help.

Karl reached into his satchel and pulled out the sphere that he filled with pyroagitating powder back in their cell. Karl tossed the ball to Spynum Begg and said, "Hold this."

Karl Lumpkin jumped over the wall and landed next to Olena. An instant later, the sphere in Spynum Begg's hands exploded. The wretched human and the Arcosauran Emperor disappeared in a burst of smoke and flame.

The explosion did not stop the bridge from folding into place. The Spinolock paced back and forth impatiently as the beams continued to slowly lower.

"I'm going to try the portal. Be ready," said Karl. He dashed over to one wall, searched in his bag for a piece of charcoal and then drew an unusual pattern on the wall. He raced over to the other wall and matched the design. Then Karl came back to stand in front of Olena as the last of the beams lowered into place.

The Spinolock charged.

Karl spoke rapidly in a foreign language and made a few quick and unusual hand gestures toward each symbol. As the Spinolock lumbered across the bridge, the symbols started glowing bright red. A white bolt of light shot out of each and expanded to make an enormous wall, separating them from the enraged monster.

Olena could not watch and covered her head with her arms. She squeezed her eyes shut and heard the Spinolock's roar. She felt its breath blow across her entire body, much closer than she ever wanted. Then Karl screamed.

Karl's voice vanished in mid-yell. The pounding sound of the Spinolock's feet stopped as well. For a moment, Olena could only hear a loud hum that must have been Karl's portal. It grew louder then stopped with a whoosh. No one else made a sound. The Arcosauran audience must have been as stunned as she felt. Then they burst with outrage and panic. It sounded like a stampede in the bleachers above her.

Olena took a chance to peak. She spread her fingers wide enough to see the huge, clawed feet of the Spinolock right in front of her. It stopped short of the line made by Karl's portal. She looked to the sides and saw that both designs used to open the portal had burned away to black smears on the walls. Then Olena looked up at the remainder of the unmoving Spinolock.

It had no head. Olena could only guess that the creature stuck its head through the portal, but did not go all the way in before it closed. While the head went somewhere else, the body remained. Then the giant, lifeless body collapsed and tumbled backward into the chasm of lava, no longer a threat.

Olena could see scattered pieces of jewelry and a wooden leg that used to belong to Spynum Begg on the ground around her. She looked up at the empty balcony. Karl's pyroagitating bomb took out several other guards as well. She saw no sign of Emperor Li-Am either.

Then Olena looked around for one other missing person. She could find no sign of her friend.

Olena said, "Karl?"

Chapter 24

Amid the chaos of the Arcosauran city, Olena could not find Karl anywhere. She could only guess that he slipped through the portal of light along with the Spinolock's head. This made her wonder where the portal took them. She felt it had to be far away. Given Karl's history of magical mishaps, he could be anywhere, maybe anywhen.

Olena made her way back through the maze, hoping to exit through the door that brought her into this mess. It remained locked. Omarika offered her assistance and gave her power momentarily to Olena's voice. The force of one shout smashed the door off its hinges. After that, Olena was free to roam the city.

With the disappearance of Li-Am, the hordes of Carcharodans and Baharians apparently did not know what to do. Soldiers ran about the palace in a panic. Olena learned that word of Li-Am's defeat spread quickly across the city. Although it was a horrible way to go, Olena felt relieved by the explosion that took both Li-Am and Spynum Begg.

A lot of commotion seemed to be directed toward the front of the palace. Olena found a wide balcony on one of the higher towers. She looked far across the Brygos and her heart filled with joy.

Several Sauropods pushed against the dam with their enormous front legs. She could barely make out what was happening, but could tell they were on the steep side by the big hole. Then her vision power zoomed in to see the Parasauratitan giving orders, while he stayed with the rest of the council, safely clear of the destruction. Other Sauropods, Hadrodons and Centuru chased away any Baharians or Carcharodans that approached. Li-Am's followers did not put up much fight.

When the dam broke, a huge wave of water rushed toward the swallowing black hole. Olena cheered as the Brygos once again flowed with its full strength.

Eventually, the council made their way to the palace. Olena waited for them in the courtyard. She noticed that none of Li-Am's followers bothered her. Maybe they thought she was too powerful or maybe they were too scared about losing their leader. In either case, they deserted the palace, leaving her by herself.

Olena liked seeing the council members again. The Trisariens looked as radiant as ever, while the Sicoglitrents looked as strange. Even in the daylight that shined down through the giant mouth of the volcano, the Thyresoterns still looked invisible. The Parasauratitan looked different though, he looked a little older.

When he got close, Olena felt a tingle in her arms and up the back of her neck. She saw the yellow light dance at her fingertips. Now she understood he did give her some power and it was not a dream. Once she completed her quest, she knew the Parasauratitan needed back the gift he gave her that night in the circle of stones.

The glowing golden energy drifted from her. She watched the countless tiny stars sparkle through the waving ribbons as he absorbed the energy.

Olena did not feel any different when it stopped. However, the Parasauratitan actually looked younger than the first time she met him. She guessed maybe it was her turn to share her power with him and she did it happily.

He said, "You have done a great thing today. I only regret that we did not agree to help you sooner. Your friends were quite persuasive."

"Kez and Sylvan? Are they here?" asked Olena. She felt overwhelmed, but happy to hear some news about them.

"Because I refused to help at first, they continued on toward Empyrean," explained the Parasauratitan.

The lead Trisarien said, "The small furry creature is very honorable and cares for you very much. His determination is immeasurable."

"From your actions, I can now return to the throne of Arcenland," continued the Parasauratitan. "We will clear this palace and city of all its evil trappings. We will free what prisoners we find and gladly accept any of Li-Am's followers that are willing to change their ways."

Knowing that Kez and Sylvan had safely returned to Empyrean made Olena want to be with them. She missed them and was glad they were safe. She did not know if she would ever see Karl again, but did not want to be in this strange city alone any longer. Olena quickly tried to open a Walking Portal. A small triangle of light formed and then disappeared instantly. It excited Olena to see even that small improvement without Karl or the Parasauratitan's energy.

The Parasauratitan offered to arrange transportation for Olena. She gladly accepted a ride across the volcanic fields on the back of a Sauropod. Accompanied by the three Trisariens, the mighty creature carried her to the border of Arcenland in a short time.

Phix found them at the edge of the Unending Desert.

"Excuse me," Olena clicked her tongue against her teeth as she often did. "Did a stone giant and a quzzak come this way?"

"I personally delivered them to the Infinity Temple," said the desert guardian. "Can I do the same for you?"

At least, it sounded like Kez and Sylvan were safe. She thought once she was free from Li-Am that they could stop at the temple if they had not already passed it. Maybe, she hoped, her magic worked and Kez received her thought like he had a few times before.

Olena bid her farewells to the Trisariens before sliding down the Sauropod's tail to get to Phix. Then she climbed up on his lion-like back, careful not to touch his pointed tail. She enjoyed the ride across the desert on his sun warmed fur. It made for a peaceful trip which allowed her to sleep briefly on the way back to Hierakonpolis.

Chapter 25

Olena awoke as Phix passed along the main street that led to the entrance of the Infinity Temple. Everyone cleared a path for them and many of them bowed. Phix stopped at the palace gate, still guarded by two cobra-headed men.

"I must return to my place in the Unending Desert. I am glad you found a resolution in the south," said Phix.

"I have a feeling we may begin to see more travelers in your desert, but no more invaders," said Olena.

"That is good news," said Phix. Then he left with no other words.

Apis greeted Olena right inside the gate. She walked with the black cat to the main chamber where Kez and Sylvan waited for her. The old quzzak leapt at Olena and hugged her tightly. Sylvan sat on the armrest of the throne, his Rockhorn body stood against the far wall.

"I'm so happy to see you two," said Olena.

Sylvan started to speak. Olena almost forgot what his high pitched voice sounded like.

"Your Majesty, it is an honor and relief to see you again," said the little wooden man. "What of the alchemist, Karl Lumpkin?"

Olena wanted to cry, "He's gone, but he saved me."

"Perhaps his disappearance would explain why the Rockhorn stopped responding," added Sylvan.

"Do you think I can make it work?" asked Olena.

"I would be willing to try for you," answered Sylvan. "For now, we would like to know of Li-Am and the Arcosaurans."

Olena told her friends everything that happened after they separated. Then Kez recounted his and Sylvan's journey. He ended by telling of their emergency meeting with Horus.

The man with the hawk's head said, "On the word of your friend, we have raised an army and even now prepared to leave, except that you were spotted on the Unending Desert. You have the respect of many that I believed would not want to fight again."

"Thank you all so much," said Olena.

"Did the small hawks return with you?" asked Horus.

Olena forgot about Captain Aeran and the Guardian Hawks! She did not see them after they left to complete their mission. She did not even see a sign of the Alkonost egg in Li-Am's palace. After her own experiences, she did not think about the tiny birds at all. This made her feel awful. She hoped they were safe.

That evening, at dinner, Olena showed off her Bronze Ring and proudly told about the Inhabitants. She had promised to help them and hoped maybe Apis or Horus might have some ideas on the subject. Sylvan watched over the occasion from his Rockhorn body. Olena's magic at least helped him.

It seemed that her magic started to grow. For a while, Olena believed her magic only worked through her connection with Karl. She feared her abilities might vanish the same as he did. Luckily for now, the abilities seemed to be with her. Returning the Parasauratitan's power did not seem to diminish her magic either.

No one at dinner had any suggestions for the Inhabitants. Olena turned the ring over in her hands. She wished she could do something. Then she saw something she had not seen since the first time she held the ring. When the Prismata gave it to her, a face stared out at her from the shiny inside surface of the ring. She now knew this face to belong to Ogustus. Olena rolled the ring across her palm and could see Omarika, then Ovara too.

The ring began to vibrate which made Olena drop it. The bronze clinked against the stone floor. It rolled to the open area in the middle of the dining room, not far from where Queen Isis fell. Olena thought she could still see gold dust in the cracks between the tiles. Suddenly, three figures burst from the ring like they were thrust out of a pool of water, but no one got wet. Ogustus, Ovara and Omarika showed no sign of being bronze statues. For the first time, Olena saw each of them in their natural form with her own eyes. Then she noticed the ring on the floor. It seemed to have lost some of its shine and luster. Because of this, Olena knew the Inhabitants were finally free.

"You freed us," said Ogustus.

"I didn't do anything," said Olena.

"It was your magic, liddel lady. I doan doubt it," he insisted.

Olena did feel different since leaving Arcenland. She wished she could thank Karl for helping bring back her magic. Everything felt so confusing now.

"I don't know what I did different," insisted the young queen.

The big man smiled, "For the first time since I was trapped, you are the only wearer of the ring that used it for good. I might guess that your benevolent deeds helped us too."

Olena introduced the ring Inhabitants to everyone in the room.

"This is Omarika," she said.

"Now that I am free, please call me by my true name, Marika Lantisphere," whispered the elf.

"What is your true name?" Olena asked Ogustus.

"Ogustus will do fine. That other name is better left in the past," said the jolly man. He flicked the end of his thick mustache with the carved handle of his cane. Then he winked at Olena.

"You can still call me Ovara," said Ovara. "I kinda got used to it."

Horus froze.

"Is it possible?" he asked. The bird man did not look away from Ovara.

"What is it?" asked Olena.

"Why are you staring at me?" from Ovara.

"Apis, have we found her?" Horus asked the cat.

The ancient black cat studied Ovara. He walked close to her and rubbed against her leg. His tail curled and he purred deeply. He walked away from her.

Apis finally said, "I believe the new Queen of the Southern Valley has been called."

"Of course, we will not know for certain until she stands in the throne room of the crystal castle, but the signs are there. Until then, I am at your service, Queen Ovara," said Horus. "Long live the Queen of the Southern Valley."

Everyone, including Olena, bowed to Ovara.

"What are you talking about? Is this some kind of joke?" asked Ovara. She did not like being teased.

"It is no joke," said Ogustus. "Those in service of the queen know one when we see one. I could not recognize it while we were enchanted, but now I see it."

"And you have definitely been called," added Marika.

Ovara looked pleased with herself. Olena ran up and gave her a hug. She could not believe the amazing coincidence. If Olena had never left Castle Empyrean, then Ovara might not have ever had the chance to become queen.

"You have to come to Castle Empyrean with me right away," Olena said.

A rumbling sound interrupted their little celebration. Olena could feel a vibration under her feet. It shook hard enough to knock glasses over on the dining table.

"What is that?" asked Kez.

"Abydos," said Horus and Ovara at the same time.

"The Brygos has returned," said Apis.

Everyone looked overjoyed. It took a surprisingly long time to wind its way across the volcanic fields and under the city, observed Olena. She now wanted to see the river flowing at its best.

"Let's go watch," she said.

The party quickly travelled through the city. Crowds parted as the two queens passed among them. They took a direct route that led them to the wide entrance of Abydos.

Olena recalled the feeling she had the first time, of the darkness beckoning her. She did not get that same feeling this time. Instead, all she could feel was the ground shaking.

"Get out of there!" yelled Ovara.

Olena followed her gaze and spotted three kids playing in the water at the entrance of Abydos. They looked like the same orphans Ovara helped in the alley by Karl's house. Far down the slope, the children did not appear to hear Ovara's warning or the sound of the coming flood. They actually looked happy splashing each other in the meager stream.

Marika started to run down the long slope, but Ovara said, "Wait. Let me try."

Soon-to-be-Queen Ovara pointed with her hand similar to how Queen Isis used to move objects without touching them. Olena remembered Isis saved her with this technique the first time she used her Walking Portal. If Isis had not lifted her with magic, the Friesian horse Tihi would have trampled her.

Ovara could not lift any of the children, let alone all three. However, she did manage to knock one over with her power. Olena guessed her magic was too new. Then Olena thought to grab her hand. Maybe, she hoped, the two of them together could save the orphans.

When Olena grabbed Ovara's hand, the new queen looked surprised. Then she smiled and they both concentrated on the children.

The rush of the coming river grew louder. Olena could see the tremendous wall of water filling the entire tunnel that led into Abydos.

First, one child lifted into the air. Olena could not watch and squeezed her eyes shut. She heard Kez yell," You've got them!" Then she felt a spray of water as the river crashed into the bed and continued past them.

Olena opened her eyes to see the three orphans sitting on a stone ledge above what used to be a wide cave mouth. Now, water filled the entire width of the tunnel and the Brygos flowed north with great speed.

"Thank you," said Ovara. She hugged Olena in a surprising show of emotion.

"Can we follow the river?" asked Olena.

Horus said, "I will send messengers ahead to warn the villagers on the shores of Lake Nata Playa. It will take some time to fill the lake, but I believe the River of Life has the power to once again flow all the way to Castle Empyrean.

"I have one situation to look into before traveling, but after that, I will be ready to go north," said Ovara. She led them back to the marketplace.

As Karl previously explained, the ugly statues on the four corners now had cracks in them. All four seals split in various ways. Mostly, it looked like something had hit each one from underneath. The impact sent fractures up the base of each statue.

"They are still holding the Forgotten Evil's lieutenants, for now," said Apis.

Olena did not like the possibility of these beings escaping. She looked to Ovara, who still seemed fascinated with the grotesque statues.

"We should go now," said Ovara. "There is nothing for us to do here."

Apis and Horus remained at the Infinity Temple. Everyone else followed the Brygos. When they made it to Nata Playa, the first obelisk Olena saw in the south poked up from the middle of the river. Water spread out on both sides of the stone column and rapidly filled the lake.

From her vantage point, Olena could see two villages already flooded and knew several more around the shores of the lake would soon be submerged. She expected the people to be sad about losing their homes, but as they circled the lake, all the people they met were celebrating.

Chapter 26

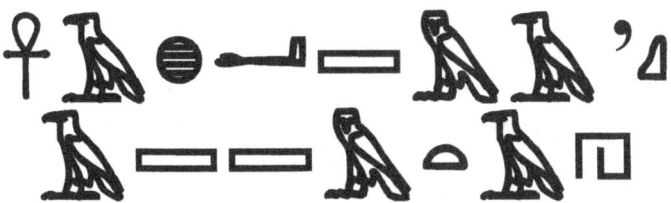

Zandria could only think about her sister. As they rode across the central plains, she worried about Olena. Unfortunately, she could only imagine terrible things happening to the little girl.

The trip across the plains would not go fast enough for Zandria. The four Friesians galloped at full gait, without stopping. Still, it seemed like the tall grass continued on forever.

Finally, a sight in the distance made her feel like they were making progress. Zandria checked with her companions to make sure they saw the object too. Adam, William and Aleta stared into the distance. Adam pointed, confirming Zandria's vision.

As they came closer, the object took on a definite shape. Zandria could clearly see the two high poles that served as masts. Then she spotted a man sitting at the tip of the prow. His bare feet almost touched the waves of grass. The rest of the land ship swarmed with busy pirates. Some worked on a broken wheel under the back corner.

The barefoot man at the front of the recently rebuilt Dragon's Wing waved at Zandria and her friends. His bald head shined under the midday sun. Mildoo Vol looked happy to see them.

"Welcome, friends," he shouted.

"A pleasure to see you again, Captain," said William.

Captain Vol rolled backwards. Zandria thought he fell off his narrow perch. She spied him hanging by his knees for a moment, and then he grabbed the beam with both hands and flipped over. He held on for a moment longer and then dropped a few feet safely to the ground.

"There is talk of a promotion," said Mildoo. "Soon, you may be calling me Admiral."

William said, "Then your efforts are going well? I know the plains' traders are not great in numbers, but last I heard you had a few holdouts."

Zandria liked the pirate's sense of style. He whipped a black bandana out of the pocket of his silky maroon shirt and quickly tied it on his head.

"One holdout to be precise," said Mildoo. "Have you ever heard of the Tripulacion de Peces Grande?"

Apparently, like Zandria, none of them had. No one responded.

Mildoo continued, "It is the biggest ship ever to sail the western plains. Captain Francisco de la Nocha Peligrosa used to be an apprentice of mine. Now he is the only one not joining the Traders' Guild. But, enough of my woes. What brings you so far south?"

"My sister," said Zandria.

"It seems the young queen has wandered off," added William.

Adam said, "We think she has gone to the Southern Valley with Queen Isis."

Mildoo Vol's smile turned to a grim frown. He said, "I hope that is not the case. I suspect the news has not reached you yet, but the Queen of the Southern Valley has passed into the twilight by the hand of an assassin."

"No!" shouted Zandria. She kicked at Fury's flanks, spurring him to go.

"Ow," said Fury.

Zandria only cared about the safety of Olena at this moment. She said, "I'm sorry, but we have to get to my sister."

"All you have to do is ask," said the Friesian General. He took off at the speed for which someday he would become legend.

"Wait," called Adam, but Zandria and Fury were already out of earshot. Adam looked to the other Friesians and humans. He said, "You coming?"

Kalis, Sulis and Stamenor immediately began galloping after Fury. They left Mildoo Vol and the Dragon's Wing fading behind them.

When the other Friesians finally caught up to Fury, they found him and Zandria waiting at the border of the Southern Valley. Only a huge dirt mound separated them from their destination. Zandria hoped Olena was somewhere on the other side of that mound. She guessed the southerners built this wall to mark the edge of the Southern Valley.

Aleta pointed at the small stream of water flowing down the center of the mound. She said, "The Brygos. The River of Life flows across all of the Southern Valley.

At the top of the mound, straddling the rivulet, Zandria spotted her sister.

"Olena," she called, both scared and relieved to find the missing girl.

The curly-haired queen waved at her across the distance with a big smile.

Suddenly, a monster rose up behind Olena. It looked as big as a Rockhorn with orange, scaly skin. It's burnt face and missing right arm only made it look more terrifying. Apparently, Olena did not know the beast came up behind her as she kept smiling and waving. It felt like a nightmare coming true.

"Watch out!" screamed Zandria.

A thunderous sound drowned out her warning. The rushing and rumbling must have kept Olena from even hearing the creature behind her. The noise revealed itself to be a flood of water smashing against the huge mound from the south. Waves ripped over the top of the hill and wonderful sprays shot up into the air. A pounding gush of water fanned out behind Olena and the monster causing a rainbow from the setting sun. Then they disappeared in the fountain. The water continued to spill over the mound suddenly turning the tiny stream into a wide river.

Zandria's heart sank watching Olena swallowed by the river. A spray of water distracted Zandria because they were too far away to get wet. Then she realized the mist hit her back. Zandria turned around to see Olena step through her Walking Portal. An instant before the portal closed, the ferocious beast followed her through in a splash of water.

"It's Li-Am," cried Olena.

She jumped out of the way as Li-Am lashed at her with his remaining left arm. The entire right side of his body looked severely burned. William blocked the swinging claws with his sword from the back of Sulis.

"It cannot be an Arcosauran," said Aleta. She jumped down from Stamenor and grabbed her spear. Adam joined her, jabbing at the creature with his short sword.

Fury said to Zandria, "Get your sister."

He galloped past Olena and Zandria stuck out her hand. She grabbed her little sister by the wrist and hoisted her up into the saddle. They rode clear of the frightening Li-Am.

Zandria turned back to see her friends holding the monster at bay. His size told her that he was dangerous. Whatever caused his burns and injuries must have weakened him enough though that he could not fight three people at the same time. Zandria expected a creature that big to easily defeat them. However, Adam, William and Aleta kept Li-Am from coming after Olena. Still, they could not defeat him.

He roared and snapped his tooth-filled jaws. The wounded Arcosauran alternated strikes between his one good arm and tail. The Friesians helped by bucking and kicking to keep Li-Am away from Olena. The monster seemed only interested in getting her baby sister.

Zandria remembered Dew telling her about the best way to keep an enemy at a distance.

She reached down for the bow strapped to Fury's saddle. Zandria quickly strung an arrow, pulled back on the bow and took aim. When she let go, the arrow flew silently and instantly toward its target.

Li-Am's head snapped back from the force of Zandria's arrow. He froze like a statue and everyone else stopped to watch. The monster collapsed to the ground. Aleta used her spear to make certain the creature was finished.

Fury trotted back over to the group. Zandria and Olena slid off his back. They hugged with a passion that they would only match two more times in their life.

"I was so worried about you," Zandria said through tears.

"I was worried about me too," said Olena.

Zandria thought she could see a change in her younger sibling. She appeared to have an air of confidence. Being close to her made Zandria feel almost like she did so long ago in the bell chamber. She could feel a power radiate from Olena that she had not felt in a long time, and only once from her sister. She remembered feeling this way the day Olena told her to search for their mother.

They still had their arms around each other as another group of people came over the mound. Zandria spotted a Rockhorn and immediately thought they were going to have another fight. Then she saw Kez riding on its shoulder.

"It's okay," said Olena. "That's Sylvan."

"Ka," said an unbelieving Zandria.

She did not know the three other people, but Olena quickly introduced Ovara, Ogustus and Marika. Zandria thought the elf looked like an older version of Dew, except with blond hair.

"Ovara is going to be the new Queen of the Southern Valley," said Olena. "It's a long story and I have to tell you about Karl Lumpkin."

"Where is he?" asked Adam.

Olena said, "I don't know. He saved me, but he disappeared. We're also missing Captain Aeran and a few of his Guardian Hawks."

Chapter 27

Olena may have thought Aeran was lost, but he knew exactly where he was.

After the others left with Gusk, the hawks decided to enter the Arcosauran city through the top of the volcano. They spiraled downward, studying the layout of the city. Aeran decided they could search for the Alkonost egg by dividing the area in four and each covering a section. Then they would meet at the palace, which seemed like the most likely place for the egg anyway.

He wanted to be thorough, but Aeran did not waste much time flying over the outer reaches of the city. He wanted to get to the palace quickly.

He had one close call with a Majungahan. The saddled Arcosauran seemed determined to make a snack of him. The two-legged creature jumped after him enough times to buck its lizard-like rider onto the ground. Its feathered head came too close to Aeran's feathered tail. He decided to gain some altitude in order to avoid further encounters.

The Captain circled the palace in time to see Olena trapped in a maze. The biggest Arcosauran he had yet seen looked ready to eat her. Then he saw the human boy Karl set off an explosive right before he jumped into the maze.

Aeran did not think Karl or Queen Olena saw the injured Carcharodan leader escape after the explosion. Karl looked too busy opening a magic portal. Aeran watched the boy step into the portal and manage to take the giant Arcosauran's head with him before the wall of light closed.

Aeran wanted to go down and make sure the young queen was safe, but Derek stopped him.

"We found it," said the other hawk.

They flew toward an open passage of the palace. With the sudden excitement, disarray replaced order. Not a single wicked Arcosauran noticed the two birds flying through their halls. Derek led Aeran to a room that looked like a kitchen. Habrok and Bellevue waited for them on top of a cabinet.

In the center of the room, Aeran saw the long desired object of his quest. He did not believe this day would come. It felt like he searched for the Alkonost egg for ages. Finally, he would rescue it.

From the size of it, Aeran thought all four of them could easily fit inside the powder blue shell with room for a few more miniature hawks. He had no idea how they were going to carry the egg.

The birds spent quite a while trying to decide how to lift the enormous prize. It looked like the Arcosaurans were preparing the egg for a feast that would never happen now. The cook had nestled it snuggly amid some decorative greens on an ornate platter. Aeran wondered if the egg would roll off if they moved the platter. He decided to try.

"Everyone, grab a corner," said the Captain.

The four Guardian Hawks each snagged a corner of the heavy platter. They flapped their wings and struggled, but finally they lifted the platter, egg and all. Aeran thought they could have knocked off some of the other food to reduce the weight. He believed that would have made the egg less secure though.

The hawks labored to carry the platter down the hall. They flew close to the ceiling, avoiding the panicked Arcosaurans running around aimlessly. When they found an open window, Aeran steered them straight up toward the mouth of the volcano. From this height, Aeran spied Olena safely riding away on the back of a friendly Sauropod. Then he saw other Sauropods smashing a great dam that allowed the huge lake to drain away from the city.

The climb up to the rim of the volcano would be remembered as the most difficult flight any of them would ever do. The journey across the volcanic fields and the Unending Desert combined would seem less difficult.

As they completed the arduous ascent, Aeran noticed one other thing. Now that the water flowed out of the volcano, the giant cauldron of lava bubbled harder. Before they cleared the rim, he saw the palace sinking into the molten rock. Aeran guessed the huge lake and constant cool temperature of the water kept the lava from overheating. Without the dam, the lava could not be controlled. Thankfully, he saw the friendly Arcosaurans escaping the same way Olena got out earlier.

The four hawks left the Southern Valley carrying the precious Alkonost egg between them. They stopped occasionally because the weight affected their air-speed velocity. In the end, they followed the rapidly flowing Brygos River across the central plains all the way back to Castle Empyrean.

Chapter 28

R age.
Li-Am could only feel rage.
She left him in the grass, staring up at the sky with his one remaining good eye.

A little girl.

A little girl took everything from him and this made him furious. She took his throne. She took his land. She took his arm. In one final insult, she took his left eye. He did not care if someone else fired the arrow. She caused it.

Li-Am stayed on the ground, feeling his life slip away. He wanted only revenge on the Queen of the Eastern Sky. He knew that would not happen now. They rode off across the plains, assuming the fallen emperor had met his end. Four birds flew overhead, carrying something.

Li-Am would not give up that easily. He defeated the Immortal Parasauratitan. He choked the River of Life for three hundred years. He even escaped the explosion that destroyed the sniveling Spynum Begg. The wounded Carcharodan broke the spell that held back the volcano in order to destroy his own city.

Then he followed the little Queen north. At least the magic that hid him from the desert guardian remained. In Hierakonpolis, Li-Am watched them at the mouth of Abydos. He wanted to strike then, but decided that two queens might overpower him.

When he finally took his chance for revenge, he planned for the surging river to finish them both. Once he ended her reign, he had no other reason for being. Li-Am did not expect her friends to come to her rescue.

Sadly, he realized, he had no one to come to his rescue. That is why he now laid there waiting for the darkness to come.

Something else arrived before the darkness did though.

Li-Am felt something tickle his foot. How strange, he thought, that he could feel something like that. He could not even remember being tickled as a hatchling. He would have laughed aloud except that his injuries made him too weak even for that.

He tried to discover what cold wet thing brushed against his leg. He felt it move up his body and linger on the spot where his right arm had been. At least, the visitor did not press into his seared flesh.

The shape eventually moved close enough that Li-Am could see out of his right eye. He did not move his head because of the pain in his left eye. The arrow felt impossibly deep and he wondered how he could still be alive.

His visitor appeared to be some hairy, four-legged creature. Li-Am did not know the humans well, but this animal did not come from the Southern Valley. It would have been out of place with its thick, muddy fur. He could tell it was not quite as big as a Majungahan, but larger than a jackal. The creature licked his face and Li-Am wanted to punch it away. That brought his mind back to his missing arm and his rage.

He thought the girl had taken everything from him. Now he realized a worse fate. Some worthless creature planned to eat him while he still lived. Then Li-Am felt another creature nosing his left leg.

With all of his rage and adrenaline, Li-Am could only mutter out one word. He pleaded, "Tawakafa."

An old voice, not his own, creeped into his ear holes. "Yes my pets, you may stop now."

Who stood over him now? Li-Am wanted to know, yet he did not have the strength to even lift his head. If this person came to destroy him, she would have an easy time of it. If she came to help, then she better hurry, he demanded in his head.

The old woman leaned into his fading eye line. He could see her worn features and tattered rags that passed for clothes. She pulled her shawl back from her head and stared at him.

"Do what you want hag," murmured Li-Am. He despised humans and learned a few unkind names to call them.

The woman reached into a pocket of her long shawl and found a small bottle. She poured the liquid contents into Li-Am's mouth. He could do nothing to resist. Where coldness had encompassed his three remaining limbs, he now felt warmth.

"I am no hag," said the woman. "I am a witch called Sasha. My wolves will carry you home now. To my home. We have much to discuss."

The two wolves that had been sniffing and licking at Li-Am's failing body transformed into two stocky, angry looking human men. They lifted the once mighty Carcharodan and dragged him off across the plains.

Chapter 29

Olena relaxed on a balcony of Castle Empyrean. She last stood on this same balcony with Isis. Now she shared it with the new Queen of the Southern Valley, Ovara. They watched the restored waterfall of the Brygos flow over the side of the bottomless canyon. The water disappeared into the mist far below.

As she wondered where the water went, Olena thought about the reunion of Marika and Tym. It reminded her of meeting her own mother. She never expected to see Tym cry, but he was not the only one with tears of joy. Tym said she looked the same as the last time he saw her.

The whole ride home, Zandria barely let go of Olena's hand. Olena appreciated the concern. Still, the adventure gave her a new sense of independence. She loved her older sister, but hoped this incident would make her act different.

She did not think she needed Zandria constantly watching over her.

They had a short, but beautiful ceremony naming Ovara as one of the four queens. Snow White and Cinderella welcomed Ovara as an equal. They invited her to stay at Castle Empyrean. Olena had a chance to warn the new queen of the impending and tedious lessons to come. They shared a giggle at this.

Olena knew she had changed when she said the words and the wall of thorns opened for them upon their arrival. This day marked the first time that she made that enchantment work correctly. Her magic continued to grow stronger which gave her tremendous confidence.

For the moment, things seemed to be good in Empyrean.

Looking out over the central plains, Olena spotted an unusual sight. It looked to be some sort of flying creature. Olena used her ability to zoom in with her eyes and clearly saw what approached. It made her happy to see Aeran, Derek, Habrok and Bellevue flying towards her. They carried a large egg on what appeared to be a silver platter. This sight put all the thoughts of home coming and reunion out of her head.

They told her of the destruction of the Arcosauran city. Olena could still feel a connection to the Parasauratitan and believed they were already rebuilding something new and better.

The arrival of the Alkonost egg caused much discussion and celebration. Olena learned that an

Alkonost egg could sit unhatched for years. No one could say for sure if this egg came from either of the last two twin Alkonosts or possibly some other older one before them. Snow White did tell her that the egg was only supposed to hatch by the touch of the Queen of the Eastern Sky.

Olena did not want to make a big ceremony out of it. Instead, she asked the Empyrical Wizards to place the egg in the aviary with the Guardian Hawks. She wanted it to be special for the birds that risked their lives saving it.

One evening, Olena joined Captain Aeran in the highest tower of Castle Empyrean. All of the hawks gathered around. Aeran and his nest mate, Fleta, perched on Olena's shoulders. Olena gently touched her finger to the light blue shell.

The egg seemed to light up from within. A crack formed under Olena's fingertip and spread out in all directions across the egg. Then the shell slowly fell away. Many pieces blew out the open windows of the gusty aviary.

Inside the egg lay two fledgling Alkonosts. They looked beautiful. They were twins, both with human female heads. They cooed, sounding as much baby human as baby bird. The sound warmed Olena's heart.

The Queen of the Eastern Sky still had hope for the future of Empyrean.

Solve the Mystery

Use the codex to translate the chapter titles.

About this book

A secret, wrapped in a mystery, hidden in a ring.

There is no greater loneliness than self-doubt. Olena has been Queen of the Eastern Sky for almost a year. She is surrounded by friends, queens and servants. But her sister, Zandria, is off on another adventure without her. And worse, what little magic Olena knew has stopped working.

Olena feels alone and helpless.

Then she discovers a forgotten gift from the Prismata – a bronze ring.

When she slips the ring on her finger, Olena opens the door to an ancient mystery that leads her to the far south of Empyrean. She starts off on her own adventure that reveals a new threat to their troubled land. A dinosaur-like race is preparing for war from beyond the southern border.

Can a young girl with no magic save Empyrean?

Or is it too late for Olena to solve the Mystery of the Secret Queen?

About the author

As a best-selling author and publisher, Mark has won various awards for writing and book cover design.

Growing up in Kansas, Mark graduated from Sumner Academy of the Arts and Sciences and received his Bachelor's in Film from the University of Kansas.

Mark has written under a few pen names with numerous novels, screenplays, short stories and digital series to his credit.